WARHAVEN

20 00
RS150B
#1765

WARHAVEN

A NOVEL BY

M. ELAYN HARVEY

A GROLIER COMPANY
FRANKLIN WATTS
NEW YORK / 1987

All characters in this book are
fictitious, and any resemblance to
real persons is not only purely
coincidental, but highly unlikely.

Printed in the United States of America
6 5 4 3 2 1

Library of Congress Cataloging in Publication Data

Harvey, M. Elayn (Mary Elayn)

Warhaven

I. Title.

PS3558.A719W3 1987 813.'54 87-12513

ISBN 0-531-15068-2

Dedicated to
the Seekers

I'd like to thank my friend
Kelley M. Wickham-Crowley
and my sister,
Dianne L. Baker,
for their advice and support.

MEH

WARNING:
STATEMENT OF DISCLAIMER

Dear Readers, do not attempt
to stare into the sun.
Cizrenhi Sunning is
a fantasy invention.
Do not stare at the sun.
It could result in permanent
injury to your sight.

Mary Elayn Harvey
Starwood Keep
1987

THE PEOPLE

Note: All ages are earth biological equivalents.

THE CIZRENHI

CINTHA	(cĭn'tha) Cintha Kathen Dh'exai, Nyjehnn's sister, only daughter of Jenna Dh'exai and Eathan Zal. Born at Dh'exai Keep on Cizren. Weaver and master of the Cizrenhi singing drum. Age twenty.
CHALIE	(cha'lee) Chalie Zal, female friend of Cintha. Died at Orven Keep on Cizren.

DH'EXAI	(day'zī) Matriarchal land title. Family name belonging to Nyath's descendants.
EATHAN	(ee'than) Eathan Zal, husband of Jenna Dh'exai. Born at Zal Keep on Cizren. Guardian for the Nordawv-Cizrenhi Alliance. Son of Aniet Zal and Thaj Orven. Died on Julle in the year 1175 N.C.A.
JENNA	(gen'na) Jenna Kathen Dh'exai, wife of Eathan Zal. Born at Dh'-exai Keep. Only daughter of Jenrie Kathen Dh'exai. Heir to the Land Steward title. Age forty-two.
KHAST	(cast) Khast Mornsyth, husband of LeAnn Zal. Born at Mornsyth Keep on Cizren. Only son of Willa Mornsyth. Botanist and agri-engineer for the Guardianship. Age thirty-one.
LEANN	(lee ann') LeAnn Zal, wife of Khast Mornsyth. Only daughter of Morthena Zal. Born at Zal Keep on Cizren. Geologist and potter. Age thirty.
LITA	(lee'ta) Daughter of LeAnn Zal and Khast Mornsyth. Born at Dh'exai Keep on Cizren. Died on Julle in the Rethyann Solar System in the year 1175 N.C.A.
MORTHENA	(mor thee'na) Morthena Zal, mother of LeAnn Zal. Born at Zal Keep on Cizren. Guardian for the Nordawv-Cizrenhi outpost on O'Nel-La. Age forty-eight.

NOAL	(noll) Noal Sant'kye. Born at Sant'kye Temple on Cizren. Died on Julle in 1175 N.C.A. Master weaver, teacher of Cintha.
NYATH	(nī'ath) Nyath Dh'exai. Matriarch. Founded the Dh'exai Stewardship and family line. A member of the First Emergence. Grandfather was Solon Sant'kye, founder of Sant'kye Temple.
NYJEHNN	(nī'gen) Nyjehnn Kathen Dh'exai, only son of Jenna Dh'exai and Eathan Zal. Born at Dh'exai Keep on Cizren. Sant'kye teacher and Guardian for the Nordawv-Cizrenhi outpost on Julle. Age twenty-five.
THAJ	(thaj) Thaj Orven. Born at Orven Keep on Cizren. Husband of Aniet Zal. Father of Eathan Zal. Grandfather of Nyjehnn and Cintha. Guardian and cofounder of the Nordawv-Cizrenhi Alliance. Died on Deun in the Arisse System in the year 392 N.C.A.
WILLA	(wĭl'la) Willa Mornsyth. Born at Mornsyth Keep on Cizren. Unmarried. Cizrenhi priestess—physician. Mother of Khast Mornsyth. Pledged to the Dh'-exai. Age fifty-two.

THE NORDAWV

MARCE	(marse) Marce Thirran V. Budding location unknown. Fifth-gen-

eration Nordawvese scholar, antiquities and exo-anthropology, at the Nordawv Institute of Psychic Biology. Cofounder of the Nordawv-Cizrenhi Alliance. Teacher of Nyjehnn. Age: no E.B.E. (earth biological equivalent).

THE O'NEL

BRACE	(brase) Brace TelRden. Born in Yyerlos, capital city of Toshin Cay, Southern Dominion, O'Nel-La. Keftain in the O'Nel-La Republic Space Fleet. Age twenty-six.
GRIFFIN	(grif'fin) Griffin Makks. Born in Cliise, seaport on the eastern coast of Toshin Cay. Ex-keftain of the O'Nel-La Republic. Chief advisor to the World Refugee Corps on Julle. Age thirty-eight.
RIL	(rĭl) Ril Camson. Flight-school friend of Brace. Died in the Storme Tides.

THE REFUGEE SHAULL

DEON PONT	(dee'on pahnt) Deon Pont. Born on Julle in a Refugee camp. Taken into slavery at age eight. Escaped Ringcity at nineteen. Sprint pilot and mechanic for Sanctuary Base. Age twenty-six.

DVORIK	(vor'ik) Full name unknown. Born on the WinterRing. Sent down and raised by Refugees. Commander of Sanctuary Base. Age thirty-six.
JAFFIE	(jaf'ee) Annie Jaffie. Born on Julle on a co-op farm. Separated, mother of two sons. Pilot for Sanctuary Base. Age twenty-four.
REED	(reed) Died by Eki-ji on Ringcity. Ex-operative for Dvorik, and a keftain in the World Refugee Corps.
SEYONE	(say'ohn) No last name. Born at Swan Cove on Julle to nomadic tribal Refugees. Sold into slavery at age thirteen to Mazzad Hendar. Native friend of Cintha. Age nineteen.

THE RINGCITY SHAULL

BREDHAR	(bray'dar) Bredhar Hendar. Born on WinterRing. Husband to the King's sister, Yundi. Age sixty-nine.
CARNET	(kar'net) Carnet Lanz. Born on SummerRing. Ex-second-in-command to Mazzad. Died 731 H.D.
CHO	(cho) Slave, scribe to Dern Hendar. Born on Julle. Age seventy-two.
DALT	(dault) Jessan Dalt. Born on SummerRing. Medical shield officer

and resident surgeon for the Altjia Summer Medical Center. Age forty-one.

DERN	(dern) Dern Hendar. Uncle of Mazzad, cousin of the King. Assassinated 731 H.D.
HENDAR	(hen dar') Founding and ruling dynasty of Ringcity. Prominent family of the Northern Dominion prior to leaving O'Nel-La.
KREAOC	(kree'ock) Kreaoc Tarm. Admiral of the Shaull Space Fleet. Age fifty-six.
MAZZAD	(ma zad') Mazzad Hendar. Born on WinterRing to Sanessal and Tamhi Hendar. Pack Reeve of the Jagar Fleet, Shaull Space Fleet. Age thirty.
REZAN	(ree zan') Rezan Hendar. King of the Hendar Dynasty, ruler of Ringcity. Age eighty-one.
SANESSAL	(san'es sal) Sanessal Hendar. Father of Mazzad. Brother of Dern. Assassinated by an O'Nel agent 712 H.D.
TVIA	(vee'ah) Tvia Hendar. Daughter of Yundi and Bredhar Hendar. Heir to the throne. Age thirty.
YUNDI	(eun'dee) Yundi Hendar. Sister to the King. Wife of Bredhar. Mother of Tvia. Age sixty-two.

Note: a complete vocabulary of alien terminology will be found at the end of this book, commencing on page 249.

THE RETHYANN SOLAR SYSTEM (NOT TO SCALE)

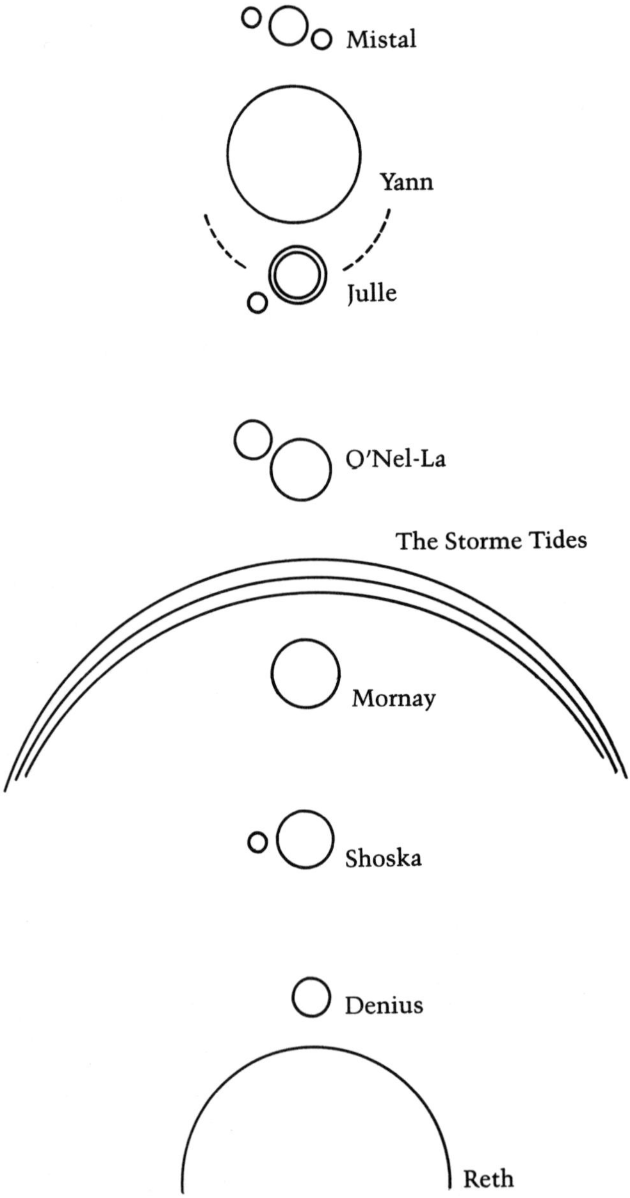

UNIVERSAL TIME LINE— RETHYANN SYSTEM

(The following information has been provided by the Nordawv Galactic Archives.)

21,315 O.E. (Old Earth)*	**4788**	Formation of The United Continents of O'Nel-La
	4964	Orbitbase I founded on the Moon
Year 1 Nordawv-Cizrenhi Alliance (N.C.A.)	**4977**	______ **21,124 O.E. (B.C.)**
	4989	O'Nel-La divided: Northern and Southern Dominions
First Cizrenhi Planetfall on O'Nel-La **184 N.C.A.**	**5161**	First Southern Dominion settlement of the Storme Tides
	5188	First Northern Dominion settlement of the Storme Tides
Marce arrives on Julle to observe **473 N.C.A.**	**5427**	Founding of the Hendar Dynasty, year 1 H.D.
	5450	First habitat constructs of the Ringcity around Julle.
	5592	Completion of Ringcity.
First Planetfall of Cizrenhi on Julle **624 N.C.A.**	**5601**	______ **20,500 O.E.**
	5807	Beginning of the Tidal Wars.
Nyjehnn's Planetfall	**6150**	
1181 N.C.A.	**6158**	present time, 731 H.D.

**O.E. is Nordawv designation, Earth's term was B.C.*

WARHAVEN

PETAL THE FIRST

THE STORME TIDES—
YEAR 731 H.D.
(HENDAR DYNASTY)

Active resistance provokes them, so you must resist passively.

It was the first directive of the O'Nel prisoner of war manual. Keftain Brace TelRden never thought he would need the advice, but he was wrong. He stood in a bare holding cell on board a Shaull military star cruiser while two guards of slave rank took away his rank rings, his uniform, and his freedom.

They beat him until he was weak and confused. They dressed him in a gray prisoner's jumpsuit and slippers and left him to his imagination. It was an expected ploy, well documented in the manual. Brace used the time to mentally replay his latest flyball game. His team had lost; things hadn't been going well lately in his life. But by the time higher-ranked guards came for him, he knew why his team had scored so low. They'd been timid on their recoveries. He'd drill them when he got back—when he got back. He kept repeating it like a mantra.

On the way to the bridge, Brace marveled at the metal rococo above him and the cloisonné ostentation around the hatchways. The deck was carpeted. This was a military craft, a large vedette-class Sprint and heavily armed. The contradictions told him much about the Shaull war machinery.

The guards jostled him through an ornate forward hatch and onto the bridge. He confronted an expansive view. The forward bulkhead was a space shield opening half the bridge to the sprawling brilliance of the Storme Tides, the inner asteroid belt that was the prize over which Shaull and O'Nel fought.

Reflecting light in all degrees of brightness and all the colors of the rainbow, the asteroids stetched before him like tumbling boulders in an invisible, dangerous river.

The view was framed by data monitors and other informative computer lights and shelved by a low helm console. Seated in the center was the first enemy commander Brace had ever seen in the flesh.

She remained sitting as the guards encouraged him closer. A dark hulk, gloved hands peaked in front of her narrowed eyes, she had the same short, dark hair and blue uniform as the rest of the bridge crew, but he knew that she, not the officer standing at her left, was the Pack leader. He'd heard of Mazzad Hendar, the youngest commander in the Jagar Fleet.

She spoke clearly with a backward nod of her head.

"What you are looking at will soon be Shaull territory. There's nothing you can do to stop that now. You are prisoner to the Shaull. I am Pack Reeve Mazzad Hendar. You will address me as Reeve." Her speech was precise. She signaled the man beside her.

"Mark him." She raised her voice. "Don't resist, O'Nel. It's done to all our captives. Much less cumbersome than shackles."

The guards held Brace immobile as the officer placed a hand-held pneumatic device against the back of his neck. Brace clenched his teeth against the stab of pain, and his eyes smarted. The officer left and the guards stood at ease as the Pack Reeve spoke again. She sounded almost happy.

"At last we have a live O'Nel. Experience has taught us what poor subjects you make for interrogation." She stood and turned to the view. She was still a hulk.

"However," she continued, "your presence here, now, raises a few questions that need answers." She held up a pen-slim instrument, twisting it between her leathered fingers. "Let's start with what I already know. You're of keftain rank, which means you're ship-linked." She turned finally and sat on the edge of the console. "So, where's your ship?"

"I'm alone."

"I'm alone, what?" Mazzad pressed the end of the pen.

Brace was seized by a brief numbing pain in his arms and legs. He rubbed his hands together, staring at the pen with complete understanding. "I'm alone, Reeve."

"You state the obvious," she sneered. "You were alone when we caught you in the Project caverns. How did you get there? You certainly didn't walk."

"I'm alone, Reeve." It was technically true. He'd sent his Starfish to camouflage itself against a nearby asteroid. They'd never find it. "I didn't expect to run into you." That was also true. He hadn't believed the reports of a new Shaull base.

Mazzad smirked. "Yes. We made quite a show of retreating. It never fails to amaze me that you O'Nel believed it. These three years of truce have been very beneficial. We've worked hard."

A call tone interrupted her from the console. She opened the circuit. "Yes, Carnet?"

A male voice answered. "An urgent message from the City, Pack Reeve. It's coded private from Grandarch Hendar."

Mazzad was surprised. "From my uncle? Download it and stay on line." She turned back to Brace. What was a blush-cheeked boy like this doing in the war? He looked too young for a pilot.

"We'll continue later. Meanwhile, I want you to think about this." She pressed the pen again.

Brace stiffened, his head and back arching and every muscle knotted with pain. His breath came in rapid gasps. She let up and he folded toward the deck. The two guards held him upright.

Mazzad approached. "That was a rather low setting. Higher is infinitely more painful, and can kill, but don't worry." She smoothed back his dark copper hair. "I don't want to kill you, yet. I'm certain you have many useful things to tell me." She signaled the guards. "Take him to an aft cell for now."

They escorted the dazed prisoner roughly off the bridge.

Between them, Brace stumbled and realized he was trembling. Whatever had been implanted in his head could control him, blocking his own nerve responses. This revelation of Shaull methods unbalanced him. He felt violated by its insidious power to attack from within. No amount of will could cancel it, nor training, nor POW manuals.

PETAL THE SECOND

Mazzad sat at her bridge monitor. "Run the message, Carnet." She read the scrolling lines as she toyed with the neural pen between two fingers.

> DERN HENDAR DYING. ORDERS YOU RETURN IMMEDIATELY. CHO

It was signed by Dern's personal scribe, but probably coded by him to get priority.

So, now the family had need of her, did they? Nobility or not, she hated them. None of the Hendar had given her the slightest recognition nor shown her any favor. That included Uncle Dern. With the assassination of her father by an O'Nel agent, he'd moved up to second chair to the Throne and had used his position to discredit his brother's blood. No, she had no love for her uncle. In fact, the whole family structure of obligations and calculated deferences disgusted her. She preferred the military, where rank earned its respect.

But she still needed them. If the Grandarch was indeed dying, that would place her as second heir, right after Tvia, the daughter of the King's sister, Yundi, who was herself judged mentally unfit to rule and was living at the family's retreat on the Summer Ring. Well, second chair to the Throne would fit in with her future plans.

"Reeve?" Carnet interrupted her. "Do you wish to reply?"

"Just acknowledge it."

The timing couldn't be worse, she thought. She needed to know how much the prisoner knew of their battle plans. How much he'd seen of the Project and whether he'd passed on the intelligence before his capture. This delay worried her. Surprise was crucial to success. If the O'Nel suspected . . . Well, she would advance the launch date. The sooner they had the system free of O'Nel, the faster her plans could be put into action.

Three hundred and fifty-one years ago the O'Nel-La Republic had revoked Shaull mining rights as if they owned the Tides. So the Shaull had declared war, or as Mazzad liked to think of it, they revoked their right to peace.

There used to be six chairs between her and the Throne, but the years of war had decimated the family. She saw each death as a necessary sacrifice, an acceptable bride price for the perfect consort; a Shaull binary system, an uncontested arena of wealth and power. Then she could return to star mining, smelting a fortune out of the Tides as her ancestral grandfather had done four hundred years ago. She would rebuild the empire and be free at last from the rule and social confines of a family that knew only duty and money. But for now, she could ill afford to ignore the order from her uncle. "Carnet?"

"Yes, Reeve?"

"I want the security patrols on the Sauradon Project doubled, and keep the base on surveillance alert. See to everything yourself. I'm returning to Julle in my personal shuttle. I want you to follow as soon as you can with the prisoner, and wait at the Hendar Docks. Use the auxiliary shuttle."

"Yes, Pack Reeve."

It would take about eleven hours to get home. Carnet would arrive two or three hours behind her. And how long to break the prisoner? O'Nel weren't strong; a day, maybe. It wasn't that important now, but she enjoyed interrogations. She wasn't consciously aware of it, but every prisoner wore her family's face. With each confession she forced her father to admit her right to the Hendar name, and the nightmare of being ignored and raised by house slaves faded—for a little while.

Her eyes wandered across the orbiting river of ice and rock. It was beautiful and hazardous, but that was much of its beauty. She loved risk. Maybe that's why she wasn't afraid of the family. She buzzed her quarters and ordered her female slave to pack her uniforms and be ready to leave.

PETAL THE THIRD

The trip home in a lifeboat shuttle had been cramped but uneventful. Yet Mazzad had relished it, as she did every opportunity to leave administrative duties and fly. The Oncom navigation help warned her of approach, and she slid into the pilot's pit as they neared Julle's moon. They skirted through its dark shadow and saw the planet's night side, looming like the black hub of a wheel. The orbital city was its blazing, silver rim, rotating in perfect balance at the equator. Closer, she could distinguish the individual lights of a thousand towers and a thousand cores beaming out the pride of the Shaull's first conquest, their own nursery world. The City was proof that they were meant to rule the stars.

Mazzad approached the summer half of the Ring and checked her braking. Her ship was automatically scanned and cleared. She matched orbital speed and berthed into the Hendar Docking Bay. It took twenty minutes of tense entry work; she was finally moored and sat relaxing for a moment, gazing out the forward shield.

It looked as if there was a reception waiting. She recognized six tall, black armored guards, Rezan's personal bodyguards, and raised a puzzled eyebrow.

In a vermilion cloak, Seyone, her slave, disembarked first, as was the custom, in case of treachery. She waited meekly at the foot of the ramp. Mazzad came down and was greeted by Cho. He was patrician in his features. His robe was long. His head was bald.

"Welcome home, Pack Reeve." He bowed low. "The Grandarch wishes me to escort you to his pavilion."

"For this you need the King's guards?"

"They are offered as a sign of his good faith. Shall we proceed?"

Mazzad fell in step behind Cho. The guards, with their obsidian visors, flanked them, their weapons at the ready. She looked inside the visor shield of the leading guard, studying his 360-degree display view of the terminal in red neon grid and the constantly updated data readouts. It must take perfect concentration to stay alert to all that. No wonder they never spoke.

She noticed Cho was nervous. And the King needed to prove his good faith by providing a security escort within the Hendar Tower? Something was wrong. She was glad for her personal weapon strapped under her arm.

They crossed the wide terminal mall and entered a spacious outer elevator. The city lights rushed up to meet them as they descended a kilometer to the rim surface and stepped out on the enclosed Summer Plaza. It was white stone and green mosaic undcr thc lanterns and divided into avenues by raised beds of dark trees and flowering hedges. The plaza was empty and their boot heels clicked and echoed in the night.

The Grandarch Hendar's red lacquered pavilion gate stood at the end of the southern avenue. Light spilled from two immense filigree censers guarding the open courtyard gate. The King's guards accompanied them to the pavilion steps, then arranged themselves in a defense line between the censers, facing the plaza. Cho continued across the courtyard, through huge bronze doors, and into the palace. After a backward glance, Mazzad, with Seyone like a timid shadow, followed.

The palace was brightly lit. They crossed the malachite ballroom floor and mounted wide gold stairs to the rose-carpeted living quarters. Cho led her to the end suite and went in to announce her.

"Find the kitchen," Mazzad said to Seyone. "Bring me some dinner." The young girl bowed silently and left. Cho appeared and motioned her inside.

The room was darkened as she expected, but smelled of fresh antiseptic and blood. She approached the high bed.

"Is that you, Mazzie?" It was a dry-reed voice.

A deep chill went through her. No one had called her that for over twenty years. Then she saw who lay in the bed. She turned to Cho. "What kind of sick joke is this?" She demanded. "This is my old house slavc. Whcrc's my uncle?"

A weary voice from the dark corner behind her

said, "We had to be certain of your loyalty. I'm not dying of the croup; an attempt was made on my life."

Cho lit a lamp, and Mazzad saw her uncle bundled on a chaise. His eyes were sunken and dull, but the broad hand outside the brocades was still vigorous and fidgeted like a trapped animal. It touched the weapon in his lap. "I was pepared to use this."

"Of course, I'd have done the same. When did it happen?"

"Two days ago. I've reason to suspect the family."

"That explains Rezan's guards." She removed her gloves.

The Grandarch made a brushing motion. "It wasn't Rezan. He'd have nothing to gain." His voice had lost some of its power.

"Yes, I'm the logical suspect. I could've paid an assassin to take you out of my way. But, I didn't."

"No. Come. Sit." When she had sat in the chair beside him, he continued. "No, you would've done the killing yourself. And you wouldn't have failed."

Mazzad smiled despite herself. She found her feelings softening toward the old warrior. "I didn't realize you knew me so well."

"You're my only niece." He closed his eyes. "I've put you in danger, ordering you home." He looked at her sadly. "But I had to warn you. I think you'll be next."

The idea that her life was at risk wasn't news. That it concerned Uncle Dern was a surprise worthy of her skepticism.

"Why bother to warn me, after all these years of nothing from you, after what you did to Father's name?" She straightened.

He laid his head back on the high pillows and took a careful breath. "It's true. I had no love for

Sanessal. He was a hedonistic, ruthless bastard. That's why I got you a commission in the military when you were five, to get away from them." He looked at her. "Everything I've done, Mazzad, has been for the sake of the Monarchy." He held out his rank rings. "Here."

She took them, as he struggled to breathe. "Watch your back, Mazzie . . . and the hands . . . of your friends." His gaze became opaque and fixed.

Cho leaned down. "Master?"

Mazzad reached over and closed the eyelids. "I have no friends, Uncle."

There was no movement in the shadowed room for long moments, then there came a timid knock at the door. When it sounded again, the old slave, forgotten in the big bed, lifted his bony rack and answered it.

"A girl named Seyone," he announced.

Mazzad stirred. "Tell her to take it back. I've no appetite now." She looked at the rings in her palm. They were too large, of course, but it was the rank, not the gold.

Cho spoke. "I should inform the Arch Concubine. But first, the Grandarch instructed me to give you this upon his death." He held out a sealed scroll.

Mazzad pocketed the rings and took the scroll. She slit the seal with her boot knife and opened it flat to the lamplight. The calligraphy was signed by Dern Hendar.

"He has made me his heir." She was stunned.

Cho bowed to her. "It has, of course, been recorded. May I be dismissed, Grandarch?"

"What? Oh, yes. Inform the household he's dead and call . . ."

"The physician," suggested Cho.

"Yes." She stood. "It seems you can handle things."

"Yes, Grand—"

Mazzad waved an impatient glove. "I prefer Pack Reeve." She moved toward the door. Cho followed.

"Rooms have been prepared for you and your slave."

"Is there some reason I should stay?"

"No, except to protect your life."

Mazzad shrugged it off and they left the bedroom and walked toward the stairs.

"I never knew military school was my uncle's idea." They went down. Seyone was sitting on the bottom step. She stood as Mazzad approached. "If I may borrow the guards, Cho?"

"They are for you, Pack Reeve."

Mazzad retraced her route, surrounded by her tall entourage. She felt more a target than if she'd been alone. At the Hendar Tower she dismissed them. Instead of up, she and Seyone went down, into the Cencom core. She wanted to check on Carnet's position.

At the threshold of the public lounge, she was passed by a cadet on the run. She continued across the reception area and entered the inner headquarters.

As she strode down the hallway, people made way for her. Those in uniform saluted. Seyone opened her office door. Everything looked the same as she'd left it two years ago. The marble-topped desk that had belonged to her grandfather still sat the prerequisite two-thirds distance opposite the door, the Cencom monitor dominated its left half. Nostalgia was framed and hung on the inner walls; pictures of all the Sprints she'd mastered. Her old, pre-Tidal calm descended on her. She walked across the transparent floor and sat at her desk. Her slave sat in a chair by the door. Mazzad noted that someone had delivered their bags from the Shuttle.

She took Cho's lettered scroll from her uniform pocket and read it again. Her uncle had willed everything to her including the deed to her own estate, which he had acquired at the death of her parents. In one sense, she was glad to have it back, but she wondered if she would ever be able to live there, or if it would have too many ghosts for her. She sighed and locked the document in the safe drawer.

Dawn was emerging from behind Julle below her. She looked down on the swirled pattern of clouds hugging the globe. They began to gain an underglow of faint madder and amethyst, and at the very edge of the planet a strip of apricot gold glinted on some oceanic surface. The orbital undercity ahead of her blazed as it came out of the shadow; a row of long, tetrahedron-shaped stalactites hanging from the vault of heaven. The beauty took her breath away, and she realized she had missed being home.

The door buzzed and Seyone opened it. The cadet Mazzad had seen as she entered the lounge stood in the hall.

"Pack Reeve? A message." He came in and saluted, then offered her the gram and left.

"Now what?" It was from the King. A recorded message awaited her on his private channel. She pulled her packet from an inner pocket and thumbed through the cards and tekars looking for his personal code. She'd never bothered memorizing it and had written it on the back of something, disguising it as an anagram. Ah, here—"Rear Hand Zen" on the back of an old docking ticket. It suited his nature perfectly; a "zen" was an old term referring to a sudden desert storm. One moment, everything was balmy, the next, there was sand in your eyes. Rezan was like that: secretive in his anger and swift in his revenge.

Mazzad punched the code into her monitor, substituting numbers for letters. The King's seal filled the screen, then faded. Rezan stretched his thin smile at her. He was so old he looked mummified.

"We've just been informed of our nephew's death. It's shocking to us that there's talk of an assassin. We've already begun an investigation. We shall, of course, attend the funerary rites tonight at the midnight. In the meantime, my dear Mazzad, we'd like your personal report on the Project. Please arrive in time for dinner. Again, our regrets at your sudden loss."

The screen darkened. Mazzad glanced at her wrist clip. Dinner? She added time zones; it was early evening on the other side of the world. This time of year, the King lived on the WinterRing, and it took an hour to get there on the Tube, the same if you went by Sprint, what with braking and docking. She would have to leave immediately. That left her no time to check on Carnet. She felt like breakfast, but dinner would have to do.

Mazzad decided to stay in the public eye; it might be smarter. If there was an assassin out there with her name on his list of things to do, at least the public system would be unexpected. She hated to ride the Tube, and everyone who knew her knew that.

She signaled a Cencom aide. The same young cadet appeared on the monitor. He must be a new member of her staff.

"Yes, Pack Reeve?"

"I want an update from my field second. He's on his way here in a shuttle. Should be about an hour out. Send it to me at the King's Winter Palace."

"Yes, Pack Reeve."

She switched off and stood. "Seyone, take the bags to my apartment and wait there. I should be back this afternoon." She handed her the tower card from her packet and hurried out.

19

Seyone bowed to the closing door. She looked down at the card, then at the bags, then down further, to the surface of Julle. The careful slave mask she wore in Mazzad's presence cleared away, and a look of terrible longing transformed her features. She no longer seemed a docile girl, but a woman anguished by the loss of her beloved.

PETAL THE FOURTH

Down and down, mesosphere, stratosphere, biosphere, down to the abused and abandoned geoidal plane, where only the unfit or the unwanted were left to live out their dust-choked years as best they could.

Along with the unknown.

The star nomads from Cizren awaited the dawn as the starving wait for food. They stood like sentinels on a high, snow-dusted mountaintop, on the open ruins of an ancient temple fane, three women and two men in long, hooded donners.

At the first fiery spark of the sun on the jagged horizon, the five, in unison, dropped the hoods of their cloaks. Their hungry eyes imploring, their hands reaching, they began to feast on light. They drank the sun's energy into the depths of their ebony eyes, welcoming its bright food as they'd done every dawn of their lives Outside, hoarding what they could before its alien light became too intense for their fragile retinas.

They looked human, yet like doves emerging from raven shells, they shone a wonder of something more. They all had hair the color of platinum and cream and the sun played invisible electric fingers through the long strands of it, making them seem to be standing against the power of the wind. But they were not; it was the power of the sun.

The fair skin of their faces glowed now, as they breathed deep, the flooding light singing down the neural pathways of their bodies, recharging, restoring, strengthening them, birthing them anew. It held them breathless, suspended in a timeless golden ecstasy between earth and sky. Expanded beyond individual identity, they became sunlight, became its song of giving, and knew again the peace and order of creation's purpose.

They rested in that joy and forgot this was not their parent star. The Cizrenhi had come to Julle over five hundred years before, during the eighth Sacred Migration. Their home sun was a star in the dense galactic core, a place they called "Inside," a womb full of stars and light so abundant that they had never known night until coming "Outside." Nor had they known this ritual of hunger until their first Planetfall. They called this rite Sunning, and without it they would die.

There was some quality of sunlight they depended upon; not every star was food. They didn't know what element of the spectrum it was; they weren't scientists, but they instinctively recognized its subtle, healing color—a color only their strange eyes could see. It sustained their psychic powers and the health of their temporary bodies. It had guided them here during Migration, and it allowed them to live on the dark worlds of the Outside.

This world became warmer, and the young Cizrenhi male who stood in the center of the group, holding the hand of his sister standing beside him, spoke the customary warning and prayer: "Zehl jerra Wey."

"Zehl jerra Wey," responded the other four. And they turned their backs to the climbing sun and watched the day advance down the mountain range opposite them.

Blue shadows became blazes of light green, dark green, and amber, with splashes of crimson from early-turning deciduous. It was the end of summer on Julle.

At the foot of the mountain their own valley still slept and their silent Keep, two stories of white brick with a central courtyard, glimmered in the morning shade. It lay in a natural meadow bordered by golden leaf and evergreens, and had a large greenhouse and an orderly garden ready for harvest. Between the meadow and the mountain they stood upon there curved a small swift creek. They had lived here for the past six uneventful years.

The temple fane was occupied and then it was not; the revived Cizrenhi disappeared, winking out between one instant and the next. A swirl of wind and snow rushed in to frost the crumbling stone.

The Keep courtyard was empty and then it was not; the five who had stood on the mountain appeared on the cold tiles. They made plans for a busy day of harvest and storing for winter.

Their hair was quiet, now, falling back in ivory veils of various lengths. The delicate boy in the center was Nyjehnn. He looked no older from the passing years, but he was changed. His hair was shorter than it once had been, only halfway down his back. He was thinner, and there was a subdued aura of restrained despair in his every move. He squeezed his sister's hand and held it close.

"I'll help you in the kitchen, today, Cintha. LeAnn wants to work with Khast in the garden." He flashed a knowing look at the pixy-faced LeAnn, standing next to her young husband. They were both sturdy and ruddy-cheeked from the hard work of fire and earth, sun and soil, and serious love.

"The kiln needs another thirty hours to cool, anyway, Nyjehnn," said LeAnn. "I'd rather work outside. It's a fine day."

Nyjehnn nodded his approval and Khast and LeAnn made a small bow but hesitated about leaving. They took off their donners as a delaying tactic. There was a matter to settle that had been put aside for too long.

Willa, the fifth member of the group, the eldest but no taller than Nyjehnn, unfolded her hands from the wide sleeves of her donner. Her face was noble, her eyes confident; the long years hadn't been serene, but they'd made her wise. She often spoke for the wishes of the others.

"We have a request. After harvest we wish to celebrate your Dedication." She raised a quick hand and made the holy sign for silence. "Before you say no again, please think about it. You've served us as acting First these six years. You've given so much of yourself to us. We want to honor you. Let us do this for you—and for ourselves. What's the wrong in that?"

Nyjehnn looked around his circle. "There's nothing wrong in what you want. I just don't feel I've earned it." He felt their disagreement before it was voiced.

"If you ask me, you have." Willa spoke for them all. "It would please us if you accepted."

He looked down at the ocher tiles, considering how best to answer without hurting them. He didn't feel worthy to receive the recognition. He didn't want to—rather he couldn't—think of taking his late father's title.

Was it that he couldn't face the truth? No, he'd faced it every day for the past six lonely years. In his mind, Dedication would seal the accusation forever in his heart. His father had died under the knife of friend-turned-enemy, but Nyjehnn had lived. And that shouldn't be the truth. Where was justice?

Willa and the others didn't understand. Yet, they were entitled to the spiritual bonding of the Dedication Rite. He wanted to please them, but . . .

Beside him, Cintha touched his shoulder. "Think about it?"

He nodded. "I will. Remind me at the end of harvest."

They seemed satisfied at his answer and left for breakfast and the day's work, except Cintha. She still held his hand.

"Let me see you?" It was her special question, asked in her special way. Not a request to see him—she could do that easily, now that he held her hand. It was a request to allow himself to be seen by her, an innocent plea for intimacy between them.

He turned to her, and she studied his features: large eyes, darker than indigo; a straight nose; a generous mouth that ended in dimples, like her own; and the wide Dh'exai jawline. Her hair was longer, but she could almost be looking in a mirror, a common trait among Cizrenhi siblings. This twinning was more a semblance of souls than mere genetic patterning, an akashic relationship that transcended parentage and time, yet Nyjehnn was older by five years. Her first Keep year had been his first Temple year. He'd come home for Star Rise and the Zho Blossom Festival called Valendon. And from the first there'd been this closeness between them that couldn't be brought to a rational account.

Except to say they were the children of Jenna and Eathan. Jenna was the Land Steward of the Dh'exai Keep on Cizren. Eathan, a Guardian in the Nordawv-Cizrenhi Alliance. Planet-held and star-held, these two eddies had an attraction to one another. In Jenna, Eathan could share a life centered in the soil and sun, the seasonal cycle of renewal that reminded all life of its immortal value. In Eathan, Jenna could share an expansive and nomadic life filled with the wonder/knowledge of stellar exploration. Migration was a cycle that unfailingly brought them together again. They gave and received, each knowing and honoring the deepest longings of the other's heart. And this honesty they gifted to their children, as perhaps it was gifted to them by their parents. It was, after all, the Cizrenhi way.

Cintha smiled deeply into Nyjehnn's eyes. She saw myriad reflections of themselves looking at each other, each pair a conscious bead on the Lady's eternal Mala. She hugged him hard.

"I understand more than you think," she said, and stepped back. The morning sun gilt the roof above Nyjehnn's head.

He said, "They've every right to be dedicated. They've earned it."

"But you can't give them something you feel is not yours."

"Yes." He squeezed her hand, relieved that she knew this and didn't judge him for it.

She became more serious. "The future is not empty."

These were a Speaker's words. They meant she had seen him in a vision. He started to ask. She shook her head. "I don't yet know the message in it, but something will happen."

He nodded. "Then I will wait."

PETAL THE FIFTH

Mazzad hurried through the Cencom core, checking the time again on a public kiosk as she strode past its screens. She was really pressed. Had the King known she was on the SummerRing when he'd made the "request"? Hard to say, at his age. Still, he would take it as an insult or worse if she wasn't prompt. She caught an up bubble and jumped out at the gleaming public administrative terminal. The morning light bounced off the chrome and clear ceramic in coppery rays from the solar filters. The open area was busy with night-shift crews just getting off work and the day shift coming in.

She wove through the crowd and pushed her way up the escalator to the loading platform. As she turned for the nearest gate, she glimpsed a figure moving up through the crowd below her. Mazzad gave no sign, but her heart thumped hard. Hell, she thought. Her uncle was barely cold; the snipe must be hungry. She flashed her ID at the scanner and entered the first car, walking to the back exit. There was an occupant in the seat by the door; she motioned him out. He noted her rank rings and moved up without protest. She sat down, loosened the weapon under her arm, and watched the faces of the boarders.

Drab green, the color she called muddy algae, that's what he'd been wearing. But a lot of people wore it, a common color in the outer, commercial ponds of the under ring. She couldn't be sure if he'd boarded or not. A warning sounded to clear the doors. She counted to ten and bolted for the exit just as they hissed shut. A few people looked startled; one looked angry.

Mazzad ran for the express and a moment later stepped out into the military terminal on the upper Ring. It was more dangerous up here for a target. Personal duels and assassinations were not unknown, and bystanders never intervened. The terminal was laid out the same as the under stations, but this one was less crowded. She rode the escalator, inspecting the movement below, seeing nothing suspicious. She made for the center gate, then swerved at the last minute and boarded the car behind. She sat at the back again, but no one seemed interested in her.

The warning blared, the doors shut, and the car moved silently and effortlessly out of the terminal. In the vacuum, it gained speed quickly and in a matter of seconds Mazzad was leaving the military sector and entering the industrial complex. The

Tube pierced towers at regular intervals; the change of early morning light was in momentary flashes, dark and bright, dark and bright. The cars had nonresponsive filters.

Mazzad continued to watch the other passengers. They read or watched the scenery or slept—oblivious of her. The larger industry towers gave way to smaller business centers, then gaps of uncompleted constructs, power stations, and finally the Tube rode the bare Ring.

It was boring and her adrenaline edge had worn off, reminding her she'd lost a night's sleep and two meals. She had to stay alert. She took her medkit tag out, peeled off a stimulant patch, and stuck it to her neck just below her right ear. In seconds her sharpness returned. It would last until she took it off or for three days, whichever came sooner. She never wore them much anymore. One time she had gone until the patch had given out; it was during an early offensive against an O'Nel podding station. The flying had been intensive; she'd used up three ships, then collapsed and slept twenty hours straight. She felt like hell for days after, but they'd destroyed the base.

The power grids of WinterRing rushed past, taking her by surprise, then the sprawl of the residential sector, complete with parks and lakes. Next the commercial towers, and the flashing dark and bright again, but this time the sun was just setting. The car slowed to a stop in the Winter Cencom Tower, and most of the passengers disembarked. A few new faces boarded.

Mazzad kept her hand on the weapon under her jacket. She watched everyone, even the mother and her kid. Her last lover had been killed by an O'Nel agent that young. She missed him, her cadet. He had been a willing sex partner who didn't mind being used and knew how to be discreet. She hadn't found anyone in the under ranks as suitable since. She never took lovers from her peers, nor anyone of higher rank. She never allowed anyone that kind of power over her.

Finally the jutting towers of the Nobility's estates and the Winter Palace came into view and the car slowed. It stopped in the Palace Green's public terminal, which was little more than a platform and a vendor's plaza at the edge of a cavernous atrium. With a waterfall and a white-water river, evergreen trees, and roaming, wild jagars; it never failed to impress her.

Mazzad sat through the exchange of passengers, keeping her empty hand on the wait button while the platform cleared. She stepped out quickly. The car left and she strode to the railing.

Cool mist from the waterfall sparked against her face. She took a deep breath of pine air and looked down a level to the forest floor. A shaggy-maned, silver jagar stood on a rock near the rapids, looking up at her. She saluted him—and the movement saved her life.

A short-range laser bolt shot under her right arm. She pushed back and dropped to her stomach, rolled toward the kiosk, drawing her weapon. The next bolt hit the screens. She ducked her head under her arms. Shattered glass flew, and smoke obscured her vision. She peered through the haze, trying to get a fix on the gunner, ignoring the frightened shouts of travelers and vendors.

His angle had been high the first shot and level the second, coming from inside the forest square. Of course, he must be on the service lift. Another bolt hit the kiosk and sheared the top. There was fire on her sleeve. She beat it out and fired blind, then ran for the lower escalator. She pushed aside a cowering body and dove head first down the moving stairs.

Another hot bolt zapped above her. She had his position now, the triangulation clear in her head. She scrambled up the descending tracks, and vaulted onto the center rail. She shot into the trees and was rewarded with a scream, the sound of breaking branches, and a thud.

The jagar below her bounded across the gorge and into the undergrowth. A moment later there was another, shorter scream. The animal appeared again, backing into the clearing, dragging his free meal. It wore a military uniform. That surprised her; it wasn't just a hired aim. Whoever was behind the hit had rank, or access to it. That didn't narrow it down much. The Hendars were a military family.

The feasting jagar raised his head to her. Mazzad smiled grimly and gave him the thumbs-up sign. She climbed down onto the ascending stairs and made her way, warily, to the royal bubble at the side of the platform. She flashed her ID again and gained an empty on its way up. She glanced at her wrist; she was going to be late, but she had a very good excuse. She would tell the King how much she admired his security, but she doubted he would get the joke. She crossed the statue-filled foyer of the ballroom and pounded on the far brass portal.

A slave opened the double doors. Mazzad marched into the dining room, her uniform rumpled and the jacket in sooty tatters. The King began clapping his hands; the other followed his example. Mazzad halted and he tapped his spoon on a crystal wine goblet to quiet the guests.

"Bravo, bravo, Mazzad, my dear. Didn't we tell you she would prevail?" He measured the faces around the table for agreement. Every diner reflected his good mood, some more genuinely than others. He stood up slowly. "Come and join us. Why you're the hit of our little dinner party, dear. We had such a good view of the whole show." He indicated a large wall screen to his left. The jagar was sharing his meal with his mates.

Mazzad remained standing, sullen and angry. So, she'd been the entertainment, had she? No doubt they had placed wagers.

Rezan came toward her, one arm extended, the other using a cane. She swore she could hear his bones crack as he walked.

He halted and said quietly, his back to the others, "Upon the word of our Throne, we had no prior knowledge of this, this . . ." His voice sounded like ripping parchment. "The security lenses record everything, and it was brought to our attention."

He turned back. "To any present who don't recognize her, our grand-niece, Pack Reeve Mazzad Hendar."

Tvia, the heir, sitting to the right of the King's place, nodded and smiled frostily. She wore a white dress uniform that made Mazzad look as if she'd just come from surface mine duty.

Bredhar, Tvia's father, on the King's left, nursed his wine, ignoring her. To his left sat the bifocaled Minister to the Throne. He was a new appointee. Mazzad didn't know his name. Across from him sat the Admiral of the Space Fleet, Grandarch Kreaoc Tarm. He raised his glass to her.

"No, don't salute here, Pack Reeve," he said, preempting her motion. "A good kill," he complimented.

"Thank you, Grandarch." Her anger had cooled a little.

"Come," said Rezan. "Sit down and eat. You must be starved." He steered her to a chair beside the Admiral and returned to the head of the table.

The sun had set behind Julle. The room was bright with gold and polished wood under the spun diamond chandeliers.

Mazzad sat and a slave brought her a plate of hot food. She was ravenous but forced herself to use her court manners.

Kreaoc poured her wine. "So, you like the jagars?"

Mazzad sipped from the water goblet instead. There were already enough drugs in her system. She thought about taking the patch off—after the dinner sparring, maybe.

"Yes, Grandarch. They kill for survival. It's the way of the Shaull." She took pleasure in thinking of her small fleet as a space-hunting pack. In fact, she'd had a jagar emblem made for each ship.

"Call me, Tarm," replied the Admiral. "Did you know your assailant? Perhaps a spurned lover? A vendetta?"

Mazzad's laugh was quick and tense. She wasn't about to reveal how much she knew or didn't know about the recent violence. Let him think she was amused. She ignored his probe and spoke to the King.

"I was followed in Summer Cencom. It was easy to lose that one. I expected to be safe in the Palace."

Tvia flushed. "Are you accusing us of negligence?"

"No. I was explaining my failure to anticipate the attack." She savored the meat, satisfied that she had a lead. Certainly not Tvia herself, but the girl obviously knew something or suspected someone. She and Tvia were the same age; maybe that made the heir nervous. It sure made Mazzad nervous. Second chair was proving as dangerous as Uncle Dern had warned.

The King patted Tvia's hand."Of course she's not accusing her own family. If you're recovered, Mazzad, we're anxious to hear of the Sauradon Project."

"I'm waiting on an update from my second, of

course, but everything was on schedule when I left. The calculations have been triple-checked, the optimum size asteroids fitted with two-stage boosters, and the orbits plotted. All we're doing now is testing and debugging while we wait for the launch window."

The King rapped his cane on the floor. "Hah, we shall celebrate. How long before the boosted meteors impact on their home world?"

"Three months."

The Minister to the Throne leaned forward, adjusting his glasses. "And there have been no signs that the Rethian Intelligentsia suspect our presence?"

Mazzad hesitated over her water glass, then took a sip and put it down. "Our probes and patrols have encountered nothing—until yesterday. We picked up an O'Nel spy in one of the Project caverns. My second is bringing him in for questioning. In fact," she pushed her chair back, "if I may check with Cencom?"

"Of course," said the King.

She put her napkin on the table and went around to the wall screen. The terminal sat on a marble pedestal next to a fan palm. Mazzad tapped in the arrival schedule. Carnet wasn't on the list so she called Cencom main tower. An officer answered.

"An honor, Pack Reeve. How may I help you?"

She raised an eyebrow over his politeness, then remembered she was using the King's channel. "I need the status on an inbound. Jagar shuttle 2442, Shield Officer Carnet Lanz."

The officer was handed a gram to sign. "We have a priority distress one. It may take some time to clear the boards." He signed, then did a double take. "What was the number? 2442?"

"Yes. A Jagar shuttle." She felt chilled.

"Seems our D1 is your man. He's gone down, Reeve."

"Down? Down where?" She swore a deliberate exorcism against the rage rising in her blood.

"Well, we're trying to locate the crash site."

"What was the last message?"

He read off the gram. "Stabilizer malfunction. No integrity."

Which meant, she swore again, they were a falling rock. Which meant the new prisoner was burned meat, maybe; Carnet was a damn tight pilot. "Is that it? He didn't sign out? Was there a zero squared?"

"No, Reeve. There's hope he made a soft landing."

She nodded. Zero squared was their private code for enemy terminated. "Send me the coordinates the moment you have them. And have the dock crew ready my personal Wing and a medic Wing. He's my officer. I'll go down myself."

"Yes, Pack Reeve." He saluted.

Mazzad snapped off. Behind her the King hissed.

"This . . . this . . . is most unfortunate. We must know what the prisoner has seen, what he may have already reported. No one must interfere with our vanquishment of the Rethians."

"Don't upset yourself, Rezan." Bredhar spoke for the first time. "The pilot probably didn't have time to signal. Take my word. The ship's in cinders."

The Minister asked, "Has there been any indication that our security was breached?"

"No. None." Mazzad returned to her place and picked up her gloves. "If I may be excused, Your Majesty?"

"Yes. This . . . must be cleared up."

Tvia said, "Uncle, haven't you forgotten something—the funerary rites?" She didn't bother to disguise the look of disapproval she aimed at Mazzad. "The family ceremonies must be attended. What will our soldiers think if we neglect our traditions for convenience?"

"Convenience?" Mazzad tried to control her anger.

Tarm came to Tvia's defense. "She's quite right. The dead must have their honor. It'll take what—three, four hours—to ready the ships? You'll need crew. And you look like you could use some rest. Your man's not going anywhere."

"What if Carnet needs medical attention?"

Tarm sounded perfectly reasonable. "If he can last out four hours, he can survive anything. If not," he shrugged.

Well, so much for their talk of soldiers and honor and the dead. It wasn't the dead who wanted the honor; it was the living—the ruling, to be precise. It was all part of their power game. And Tarm, he was so blatant. She knew what he wanted. Thanks to Uncle Dern, Mazzad now had the rank to deny him. Still, she felt trapped by these senseless hours of waiting.

"My orders, then, Your Majesty?" She faced the King at full attention, retreating to military formality; it was the only way to control her disgust of them.

Rezan turned to Tvia. "What is the funeral schedule, dear?"

"A private car will take us to the Halls of Death just before midnight."

Rezan propped himself up on his cane. "You may rest in your uncle's apartments, Mazzad. And I'll have a suitable uniform sent up. Did you not bring your slave?"

"I didn't plan to stay this long."

"Well, we must find you an attendant." He

looked to Tvia, who nodded her willingness to take care of the matter.

Mazzad was eager to be rid of them. "May I go? I find I'm quite tired after all."

"Yes, certainly."

Mazzad saluted and strode out, relieved to get away before she lost her temper and told them exactly how much she hated their cold narcissism.

PETAL THE SIXTH

Nyjehnn was a sudden brightness in the midst of the night. He stood alone on a forest-shrouded ridge, lithe and angelic with wind-tossed nimbus hair. He was dressed in soft tans and a watersilk shirt, and wrapped in a furmine cape. His feet were bare, to better feel the land. This forest was thousands of kilometers from his Keep, yet the deep secrecy of these woods flowed out to his presence, whispering his name. He recognized its voice. Tonight, it was fear. Fire ate at the trees below him.

He lunged and raced recklessly downhill toward the flames. Closer, he spotted the cause—a twisted starcraft lying in a havoc of scattered metal feathers.

He had felt it plunge from the injured sky, had come looking for survivors, led by the disturbance that was like an acid on the flesh of the land.

Nyjehnn grabbed a sapling and skidded to a stop. He projected his awareness, searching for life. The scent of pine was invaded by smoke. The fright of small fleeing creatures distracted him. He discarded the natural for the unnatural and touched a whimper of thought from within the ship. He ran through the last of the trees and plowed to a stop in front of the looming, tilted wreck.

Frantic sputterings of burning pitch assaulted his ears and furnace heat whipped his face. Nyjehnn gasped for breath and raised an arm to shield his delicate eyes. He searched the shadowed hull for an entry hatch. It was there, forward, almost buried in the smoldering roots of an upturned tree.

As he climbed toward it, a plunging branch hit the hull above him with a shower of angry cinders. Nyjehnn ducked but one stung his hand. He sucked at the pain and brushed through his kinetic hair with his other hand. He approached the hatch. Heat radiating from the ship's skin was a warning. He pulled off his cape, wrapped his hands and forced down a small panel beside the hatch. Two buttons: he stabbed both. There was a loud click and a stuttering whine, then the hatch slid halfway down.

The interior was dark with a strange smokey scent. Nyjehnn laid his cape over the hot metal door track and vaulted into the ship, rolling once and landing on his feet. He was in a passageway that stretched the length of the ship. There was an open hatch at his left. He looked inside.

A dim, overhead panel lit what must have been the bridge. He went in and checked the swarthy figure pinned between the broken command seat and ruined console. He was dead. Nyjehnn made a quick hand sign over him, then turned back and continued down the passage, checking cabins as he went.

Thickening smoke made him cough, lack of air made him dizzy; he stumbled to the last door and looked inside.

A bobbing handlight sliced the gloom. A boyish shape was pawing through a wall cabinet, throwing unwanted objects to the tilted deck.

All at once, a shuddering explosion rocked the ship violently. Nyjehnn managed to hang on to the hatch opening, but the searcher was thrown against the forward bulkhead with bone-shattering force. He screamed and slumped to the deck.

Flashes of electrical showers strobed the cabin like wild lightning. White smoke rolled along the ceiling from the aft deck. Nyjehnn stood, lurched to the rising alien, who held one arm against his side, and grabbed his good arm. Their eyes met for an instant. He saw that this being was young like him and different from the dead one. In his eyes he recognized pain and fear and the readiness for death.

"Out!" Nyjehnn shouted. "Now. Come on!" He pushed him ahead into the passageway. They both stumbled to the main cabin. The alien jerked free of Nyjehnn's grip and made for the dead pilot. With his good hand, he rifled his uniform pockets. Nyjehnn grabbed him again.

"Nothing's that important! Out!" He pulled him to the outer hatch. Nyjehnn's cape was burned. He left it and they both jumped into the roaring red outside.

A heat storm flayed their faces. Their lungs sucked at the hot empty air. The alien yelled strange words. Nyjehnn could understand only the terror on his face. The fire surrounded them.

Nyjehnn motioned him to stay calm, but panic was too close. The stranger turned back to the ship. Nyjehnn spun him around and gripped his upper shoulders, pressing his thumbs deeply into the carotids under the jawline. The alien fought against him a few moments then fainted. Nyjehnn caught him under the shoulders and held him up.

He gathered his inner energy and closed his dark eyes, forcing his mind to ignore the crackling heat, shutting out the danger. He focused his trained awareness on raising the cellular vibratory rate of the alien's body, then his own. When they were both light, he reached for the ridge above them. His mind built the distant reality, remembering the safety. Cool, moist air, green virgin trees, soft pine carpet; he stepped forward onto this high forest vision with the alien and felt the safe land under his bare feet.

He gulped the rich air and looked back down at the fire devouring the valley below, racing toward them. No rest yet. He concentrated again, transferring awareness first, then substance.

Two ridges away now, the fire was a silent sullen glower in the southeast. His companion stirred. Nyjehnn lowered him beside a mossy boulder as the distant wreckage exploded one final time and a red boiling cloud pushed aside the night. Natural lightning prodded the climbing column and thunder protested, rolling across the threatened hills. Nyjehnn smelled rain and smiled gratefully.

The other boy struggled to his knees, cradling his broken arm. He shied back when Nyjehnn reached for him.

"I didn't harm you," soothed Nyjehnn. "It was the only way to get us both out alive." He hoped something of his tone would be understood.

The first sprinkles of rain touched them. The young alien lifted his face, a long unused gesture. His thought was open to Nyjehnn: (Rain? How long has it been since I've felt rain?) The words of the thought were foreign and left a garbled echo in Nyjehnn's mind and a taste of hopeless sorrow, an emotion that bloomed a sudden kinship in him. He wondered from what tragic place this boy had come.

Nyjehnn reached gently this time and there was no objection; the boy looked close to collapse.

Nyjehnn pointed his mind west, toward the sun shining half a world away. He shifted his focus and they disappeared in a whirlwind of light, leaving only spiraling scents of smoke and singed cloth, things the forest feared. The rain fell harder.

PETAL THE SEVENTH

The amber-tiled courtyard shimmered in the late afternoon heat, and early autumn leaves curled and skittered aimlessly on the welcome cool breeze. Willa stood waiting under the shade of the second-story balcony. She waited quietly with her hands folded into the sleeves of her peach silk kimono. She wore her long satin hair in a thick braid coiled around her head. This accented a tall neck, one of the reasons Nyjehnn called her Mother Swan. Another reason came from the care she lavished on him and the others of the Keep. A red lacquered medical box sat at her feet; Willa was a Cizrenhi priestess-physician.

She watched two leaves soar, circling and tumbling each other. She unfolded her arms. He was coming back.

Two young men appeared in the center of the courtyard. One was Nyjehnn.

"Willa, help." He stumbled under the weight of his unconscious burden.

Willa hurried over and helped him to his feet. She noted the alien was an O'Nel and was surprised. He was fair, with a shag of short auburn hair. His snug gray garment was torn and smudged with black and white soot. The smell of scorched metal and rain clung to them both. Nyjehnn looked haggard.

"Are you all right?" she asked him.

"Just tired. Help me take him to my room. It's closest. And careful, I think he broke his left arm."

Willa ducked her shoulders under the O'Nel's arm and they carried him gently across the courtyard. She bent and retrieved her medical box by its strap and they continued through the wide portico into Nyjehnn's airy room. They laid him on one of the opposing beds. Nyjehnn collapsed on the other to catch his breath. Willa opened the white, leno-woven drapes at the back french doors and drew a quilt from the blackwood chest nearby. She covered the boy, then worried over Nyjehnn, testing his forehead and the tympanic pulse at his neck.

"You've hurt your hand," she observed.

"Just a small burn." He opened his eyes. "He's not hurt, other than his arm. I think the jumps were hard on him. Me too."

"Here, let me fix that." Willa sat her box atop the bed, opened it, and chose a small jar and a soft bandage.

Nyjehnn sat up as she tended his hand.

"There was a fire?" she asked, trying to draw him out.

"Yes."

The static electricity was gone from his hair now

and he looked calmer. She excused his answer, attributing it to preoccupation. Willa knew better than anyone how demanding a rescue could be.

"Oh, I just remembered. Marce wanted to see you when you returned." She replaced the jar. Well, he would tell Marce and Marce would tell her. That was the way of it. After all this time Jenna's boy was still shy and respectful with her.

Nyjehnn crossed to the tall armoire in the corner and took out a clean shirt. He stopped beside the bed for a moment, looking down at the unconscious youth. Nyjehnn was certain he was an O'Nel, and puzzled by it and, deep down, a little wary. He went on into the bath, braided his hair back, and doused cold water over his face, upper body, and feet. Refreshed, he toweled dry, changed into the clean watersilk shirt and pulled on his soft boots. He felt more himself.

He strode through the bedroom. "I'll be back as soon as I can. I think I know what Marce wants."

When Nyjehnn had gone, Willa examined the O'Nel. He might be near Nyjehnn's age, yet she thought that idea unusual for a being born under a different sun. Years were not counted the same on Cizren as they were Outside. She opened his collar and placed her palm atop his bare chest. His heartbeat was faster than Cizrenhi normal, his skin more tan. She was about to start a blood study when a gentle mind touched hers.

("Do you need any help?")

Willa answered in kind. ("Come in, Cintha.") She watched Nyjehnn's sister glide in, all luminous in a white wist and shorter work apron. They continued their quiet thoughts.

("Is it strange?") asked Cintha.

("*He* is very much like us,") Willa assured her.

Cintha touched his sleeve. ("He's injured. I smell fire and I feel danger.")

("A simple radius fracture. Nyjehnn mentioned a

fire, but he was very close-minded about it. I hope it wasn't too serious.")

("Couldn't be. My brother's mood is so much lighter than when he left.") She tossed back her ivory hair, which fell loose to the hem of her apron. ("I have a feeling this stranger is the answer to a prayer.")

("Yes. It's well that Nyjehnn's working again. It's good for us all. Help me with this suit.") Willa unknotted the lacings at his cuffs and together they eased his clothing off.

Willa saw the bruises of a recent beating, but said nothing to Cintha. She covered him with the quilt, cleared her mind, and probed his broken arm with delicate energy to move the bone back together, realigning tissues and muscles. She worked skillfully without need to further bruise or cut the skin, as her mother had taught her, as all the Cizrenhi healers were trained. She stroked his arm, testing the nerves. All was well.

Cintha remained quiet as Willa analyzed the alien's blood, immunity factors, and general health. He was in good condition. She took a cast roll from her box and began winding it on. She opened his hand to wrap it and gasped.

("What is it?") asked Cintha.

Willa felt uneasy and spoke aloud. "There is some kind of circuitry imbedded in his palm. I've not seen anything like it. Well, one cannot see it, it's under the skin."

Cintha traced her own palm wonderingly. "How odd."

The boy moaned and began to awaken. Willa finished the winding and checked the other hand. It was the same; minute gridworks that were obviously biocompatible.

PETAL THE EIGHTH

Marce was in the greenhouse behind the Keep. It was a large, humid room of towering jungle greenery, tamed tropics soaring in fanned ferns and broad-leafed trees, hanging in long vines and billowing in bushes that looked like giant yellow thistledown. It was a small attempt at a re-creation of Cizren.

The light was dazzling. It poured from the sky through the glass ceiling and walls and was amplified by various size sunballs peeking out from surrising places. They hung from the ceiling supports, and from myriad tangled vines and branches. Many lay, wet and sparkling, among the lower planting, beaming auras of misty light.

Marce stood in the center of this jungle, like an oversize chimpanzee with a drooping mustache. Except he wasn't simian; he was Nordawvese. An aged galactic anthropologist/archeologist, student of the universe and alien philanthropist. He was also somewhat of an exobotanist. He stood patiently slicing a petal from the stamen of a special plant he'd raised from seed. The mother plant grew on Nordawv, his home world, an ancient place high above the galactic plane.

He held the stalk firmly with his lower right hand, spread the leaves down with his lower left hand, anchored the stamen with his upper right hand, and cut the petal free with a sonic blade, which he held in his upper left hand. It was delicate work; the petal had to be of precise thickness to code easily, yet sturdy enough to resist accidental breakage.

Someone came in and closed the door against the cool breeze that droned, like a somewhat muted swarm of sonorous bees, outside the solar-powered vents.

"That you, Nyjehnn?" Marce held the petal up to the light of a nearby sunball. It looked perfect.

"Yes."

Marce took a silky envelope from one of the upper pockets of his blue homespun robe and put the petal away inside it.

Nyjehnn came, ducking through the lush foliage. The leaves stirred as he approached, and the sunballs twinkled like stars in an aqueous, green sky. He stopped before the stooped-shouldered Nordawv, a willowy child beside his girthy professor. He saw the petal plant.

"I had a feeling. Why so soon?"

"You're out of practice." His voice was deep and rumbling where Nyjehnn's was a soft husky tenor.

"Very true," agreed Nyjehnn. He tried to remember the last petal he'd recorded and couldn't—at first.

"Planetfall, year 3," supplied Marce.

"I don't remember."

"I made you record it. Right after your year of silence." He added the last gravely.

Nyjehnn looked away. "I don't want to remember." It was the year after his father's death.

"That's why I made you record it. It was important. It may be of great good in the Alliance archives. One never knows the true value of things at first. Take the Alliance, for instance. It's turning out to be extremely valuable for the Nordawv side." He dropped the sonic blade in another pocket and dusted his four hands. "The exchange of knowledge between the Guardianship worlds is bringing a ninth renaissance. Did you know that?"

Nyjehnn was passive, trying to adjust to the subject. There was so much in his mind that needed setting aside.

"You used to care about such things. Your old teacher may be vindicated yet." He turned and lumbered away, following the damp gravel path farther into the jungle. "But let's not talk pasts. Come. Tell me what you think of my glasswork."

Nyjehnn followed. "Of course you'll be vindicated. One day those pompous faculty snouts will be lowered and you'll be raised up." He realized what he'd just said and sighed impatiently at himself. "I mean, you'll be honored for the visionary you are."

Marce's laughter was deep, almost a vibration in the air.

"Pompous snouts . . ." He continued to chuckle as he led the way to the outer wall of the greenhouse. Here, his furnace sat beside LeAnn's cooling solar kiln.

He took a newly blown sunball off its wooden rack and tossed it to Nyjehnn, who almost didn't catch it.

"Who was the distressed traveler you rescued today?"

"He's O'Nel," said Nyjehnn, distractedly, turning the fragile glass in his hands.

"O'Nel? He's a long way from home. Should be an interesting story."

"Yes. Considering I found him in a Shaull Sprint."

"A very interesting story." He nodded at the sunball. "Is it sound?"

Nyjehnn caressed the globe and concentrated on it. It began to glow with golden light, shining like the others around them. He pulled the energy back and it darkened. He tossed it back to Marce. "Yes, of course. I think there's nothing you can't do."

"I can't place a duplicate of my memories inside an organic crystal for another to absorb and experience. Let's code this petal." He put the sunball away and took the envelope from his robe. "We can sit here." He motioned to the wood deck enclosing a pool behind them.

Nyjehnn folded easily, in lotus fashion, and Marce settled on his heavy haunches beside him. He put the unblossomed petal in the boy's waiting palm. It covered the center cross of fine lines and shone a chalky white.

"Where do I start?" asked Nyjehnn.

"Begin at the crash site."

He nodded and gathered his thoughts, plucking them from the hours behind him and holding them in the now. He touched his tongue to the surface of the petal, then covered it with his other palm. He closed his eyes and concentrated on the molecular information spreading across his tongue and into his bloodstream. It had no taste, but he had been trained to its form.

He plunged through the blossoming already starting within him and captured one cell. He expanded its crystaline structure and entered its polygonal beauty, and found himself standing in a transparent room shaped like a hexagon. The walls vibrated slightly and the rainbow sheen on them danced in rhythmic, coruscating patterns. Beyond him stretched a virgin world of empty rooms, awaiting his presence.

And there was sound in this universe, soft and hypnotic, pulsing with the vibration and falling on the inner ear like a polyphonic heartbeat. Nyjehnn chanted his memories in time with this cosmic music, starting with his view, from above, of the wreckage among the trees. When the room could hold no more, he penetrated the membrane wall like an image that grows at the side of a mirror, stepped into the next room and on to the next event.

He moved in an outward spiral, leaving those tense moments of fire and panic and rescue in his path. And as he moved he changed the structure of the rooms and their alignment with one another in the matrix of the cell. Changed forever its genetic message so that it no longer told itself, but told of this one day, this part of an hour of Nyjehnn's eighth year in Outside.

When he finished, he released the cell in the moisture of his palm and watched the chain reaction of information spread until the entire petal was restructured, coded with a perfect memory. Then he opened his eyes and his hands. The petal glowed a soft opalescent pink, the sign that it was blossomed.

Marce lifted it gently and tucked it away in the watersilk. "It's beautiful. I'll store this with the others."

Nyjehnn rested his head on Marce's ample knee. "I'm so tired," he whispered.

Marce put his lower arm around him. "It's just the coding. Take some light." He indicated a nearby sunball.

"No. I've got to get back to the O'Nel." He pushed himself up and stretched. "Willa must be finished by now." He yawned.

"Don't stay up all night teaching him to talk. Use my tutor. I put it in the library."

"Thanks, Marce." Nyjehnn returned to the jungle.

PETAL THE NINTH

Nyjehnn came back into the room and stood beside Cintha.

Willa said, "He's waking. Look at this." She held out the O'Nel's palm. "Do you recognize it?"

Nyjehnn looked closely at the biocircuitry, like a fortune teller scrying a future. "I don't see . . . oh." He stroked the skin with a finger. "It's artificial. No, I've never seen anything like this."

The boy opened his eyes and focused on Willa. Hc spoke.

Willa looked to Nyjehnn for a translation.

Nyjehnn released his hand and shook his head. "I haven't taken the language yet."

Willa closed her medic box. "Well, I'm starving. You can worry about the languages; I'll start dinner."

Cintha reached for Willa's box. "I'll help."

Willa took the box from her hand and they left.

The alien said another sentence. This one carried the common inflection of a question. Nyjehnn motioned him to rise and held out his hand to help. The O'Nel sat up, grasped Nyjehnn's wrist, stood, and steadied himself. He's my height, thought Nyjehnn. Somehow, the alien had seemed bigger. Nyjehnn attempted to step back, but the other restrained him, bowing over his hand. The unexpected ritual stilled Nyjehnn. The alien straightened and spoke a clear word, tapping his chest. He had given his name, Brace.

Nyjehnn pointed to himself and said his name.

Brace smiled timidly and tried it out. They shook hands.

Nyjehnn took quick note of the fresh bruises: the Shaull, he guessed. So, they had something in common. He decided he didn't want to know more and said, "Well, you'll have to know more than one word of Dhoran. And you'll need some clothes." He brought tans and a watersilk shirt from the armoire and showed Brace how to belt them on. "I'll learn your tongue later."

They walked out together, crossed the courtyard again, and entered the library. The long room was warm in the early evening, dim with the henna drapes half drawn. The dark wood floor was patterned in gleam and shadow, and tiers of books slept on the wall shelves amid odd curiosities.

Nyjehnn led Brace to a low counter against the back wall. On the counter sat a large cube that was part transparent chamber and part opaque crystal base. He pulled over a chair for Brace and removed a slim remote headset from its drawer beneath the tutor. He tuned the setting as Brace sat down.

Nyjehnn turned to him and tried to sound reassuring. "This is a language tutor. I've used it myself many times. I give my word. It's harmless."

Brace inspected the machine, looked at Nyjehnn, and shrugged. He reached for the headset. Nyjehnn helped him adjust the fit and stepped back. Immediately random points of light began to coalesce within the chamber. Brace watched in rapt fascination as the suspended glow started to change hues rapidly, locking into the primary colors.

Nyjehnn watched until he was satisfied with the man-device relationship, then he sat at the round study table to wait out the run. He stetched his long legs and leaned back, grateful for the chance to rest. The trip out this morning had been easy, but getting out of the fire and bringing back Brace, who outweighed him, had been almost too much. He felt drained to his very bones.

Then Marce had called him to record the mission the moment he'd returned, anxious that Nyjehnn should fulfill Guardianship duty. He was glad for the old Nordawv's care, but he knew that behind the support Marce worried about Nyjehnn's ability to cope with an Outsider. Well, didn't he have doubts about that himself? Brace was bringing them all forward again. How many times had he hoped to avoid this part of his duties, but knowing it was inevitable. He'd taken steps to protect his Keep—and himself—relocating in this alpine wilderness, hiding, waiting to face this. He'd always known this day would come.

He rubbed the bandage on his hand absently and stared out through the glass door at the darkening courtyard. The ghostly lines of an older courtyard superimposed their image. Nyjehnn warned his thoughts away, trying to stop his mind, but the haunting scenes played him again:

He was standing in that ghost courtyard, under the full moon. There was no sound on the night wind.

There was no light in the Keep. He turned, looking at the scattered, ragged mounds lying on the stone. They were vaguely familiar. As he knelt beside each death and recognized it, his heart knotted tighter with a frightful horror he'd never before experienced. He was in shock. He couldn't cry, not even when he found Lita—Khast and LeAnn's young daughter. She looked to be sleeping, under the callous moon, but there was dust in her hair and darkness in her eyes.

He couldn't scream when he found his father. He wanted to scream, to deny this nightmare, to wake up. He felt himself go small and blind inside. He couldn't bear to see it anymore. He didn't want to find his sister, it would kill him.

And then there were strange, hurtful hands upon him, dragging him across the courtyard, slamming him against the gate. The pain started and all he could remember for a long time was the pain.

Six years ago now. How many times had he punished himself with it? Would the facts somehow change? No, but he kept hoping that one day he would understand the reasons.

Nyjehnn rose and paced the library. Some had survived; six of them. Did he survive? Did he? Something of him had not, but he didn't know what it was. Sometimes he wondered if maybe he was afraid to know.

Time walked mercifully away from that night, and duty and living led him on. Duty brought him back to the present. He stopped at the window. Sundown was coming on a cleaning breeze that sent a leaf over the opposite roof. It imitated lazy flight, drifting down the wind as his life drifted in time. Ready or not, he was the First now. It was his responsibility to return Brace to his home world. As stated in the articles of the pact with the Nordawvese; "The People of the planet Cizren shall be accepted as legal members of the Nordawv Union of Planets, with all the full rights and responsibilities thereof."

In detail, article six stated: ". . . to maintain a sanctuary and rescue station at every outpost and to serve in such capacity upon request."

The fact that his father had helped to write the articles reminded him how much he was on his own now. Part of him was relieved to be facing this at last; part of him was very scared.

He glanced over at Brace. His life will depend on me, he thought. That wasn't what worried him. It was the idea that he might fail, and failure would mean more weight on his conscience, and already the burden was telling.

He sat at the table, laid his tired head on his arms and tried not to think.

PETAL THE TENTH

Nyjehnn woke with a start. It was dark, except for the faint glow of the tutor. He reached toward the sunball in the center of the table. Cintha materialized beside him, holding a tray of full cups and plates.

"Dinner," she announced. "You've not eaten all day." She set the tray on the table and placed her hand over his on the sunball. Under their palms the small globe began to radiate a soft light until they were bathed in warm brilliance. She served her brother a steaming cup of tea.

Nyjehnn started a cautious sip, when the timing hum of the tutor surprised him. He put the cup down and crossed to check the base display. The light indicated that Brace had taken the course in a little over half the normal time.

Nyjehnn detached the headset. "Brace?"

Brace blinked and looked up. "What?"

"The lesson's over. Come and sit at the table with me." He stepped back and replaced the headset in its drawer.

Brace gave the silent machine a puzzled look of respect as he stood. He turned and saw Cintha. "I remember you."

"My sister, Cintha," introduced Nyjehnn. "This is Brace," he said to her. She was unloading the tray.

"Your sister, I guessed right. You two look so alike. Are you twins?"

Cintha giggled behind her hand. "No. Nyjehnn's older." She put the last dish on the table, bowed slightly, and vanished in the middle of turning away.

Brace looked shocked a moment. "Is that how we got out of the fire?"

"Yes. That's why I needed you quiet. I'm sorry about that."

"It's all right. I shouldn't have panicked." He pointed to the empty air beside Nyjehnn. "You do that all the time?"

"No. If it bothers you—"

"No, no. I'll get used to it, I guess." He dismissed the offer with a wave of his good hand and changed the subject. "That machine . . . tutor. It taught me new language in what—an hour? How does it work?"

Nyjehnn blew on his tea. "It's a hypno-mnemotechnic savant. I really have no idea how it functions. It's a very useful tool. Standard equipment on every based planet in the Guardianship."

Brace nodded. "Yes, this planet. Where am I? Who are you?" His voice tightened. "What happened to the ship?"

Nyjehnn raised his hand to stop the flood of questions. "It exploded. The pilot's dead, I'm sorry. I'm curious too. You're an O'Nel. What were you doing on a Shaull Starsprint?"

Brace pressed his palms on the table. "Where am I?"

"You've crashed on Julle. Relax. There's no Shaull here."

"Where on Julle?" He sounded frightened.

Nyjehnn leaned forward. "Believe me, you're safe." He took a holoconic atlas from his pocket, moved a plate of bread, and set it on the table between them. He touched it and a topographical globe hung above the table in full color. It rotated slowly until the polar view descended. Nyjehnn mentally directed a pointer to a mountainous region on the north coast of the largest continent.

"We are very isolated up here and well out of scanner range of the City. We're also half the continent away from the crash site. The City can't trace you if that's your worry."

Brace sat staring at the globe's shadow on the table. "I was a prisoner on that ship. They were taking me to the City for questioning. The war's still on, you know."

Nyjehnn felt a stab of fear. He had deliberately ignored the war, had put it out of his consciousness every time it intruded.

"The Tidal Wars," explained Brace. "Don't you know? How can you live on Julle and not know about the war?"

"I told you, we're isolated up here." Nyjehnn tried to quell his panic. Brace was an escaped prisoner. There might be a search; well, they could never trace him here. He clasped his hands in his lap. They were cold and trembling. He forced himself steady. "It's by deliberate choice. Our presence must remain secret to do our work. I am a Cizrenhi and a member of the Guardianship. We normally have no relations with other races. We exist as a service and communication network for the Nordawv-Cizrenhi Alliance. It's my duty to monitor this planet only and to be ready to give aid to my people or the Nordawv or any travelers who might need help."

"Like me?"

"Yes, if you request my aid. Do you want to go home?"

"You make it sound so easy. You've never known war, have you, Nyjehnn?"

"No, not the way you do."

"I thought not. But you do know about enemies and death. I can feel it in you."

Nyjehnn nodded. "I thought you empathic." It confirmed odd certainties he'd had earlier.

"I've had training. So are you."

Nyjehnn touched the atlas, and the globe winked out, leaving the air between them dark and shadowy. "No, I'm a . . ."

"Telepath," guessed Brace.

"Yes, in a way."

Brace nodded. "Your sister, too? And the healer?"

"Yes. And the few others you'll meet here." He noticed Brace was massaging his arm. "Are you in pain?"

"No, not really."

"It's late. We can continue tomorrow."

Brace ignored the offer. "Have you ever read a Shaull mind?"

"No."

He smiled weakly. "Do you have a ship?"

"No." Marce had one hidden in an eccentric orbit, but it wasn't interplanetary.

"I don't think much of your service."

"The standard procedure is to send a message to my link on O'Nel-La. She will contact someone who can arrange transport."

"There's no place like this on O'Nel-La," stated Brace.

"You wouldn't know of it."

"Besides, no one will risk bringing a ship this far, nor expose it to such close danger. With the war losses, they're too valuable. It takes a long time to grow replacements."

"Grow?"

"The Starfish are semisentient organiforms native to our system. They spawn and live in the matter-rich Storme Tides, the inner asteroid rings. When they mature, we match them with compatible pilots. The two make the perfect tactical space weapon: a thinking ship. They're our very life. I won't endanger one to attempt my rescue."

"You mean that, don't you?"

"Yes. You're sure we weren't traced here?"

"Certain. You can rest. I'll try other contacts and find something. Do you want to go home?" Nyjehnn asked again, putting the atlas back in his pocket.

Brace sighed. "Yes. But I never thought to see home again. You don't mind if I disbelieve you?"

Nyjehnn understood his fear to hope. "No. I don't mind."

PETAL THE ELEVENTH

Brace woke with the late morning sun in his eyes. He was confused by the golden silk-draped stone of his surroundings. Then he remembered yesterday. Yesterday? It felt like it, but he wasn't sure. He'd lost the track that time and place measured out as his life, and he felt adrift in his own skin. He wasn't home; he was on Julle; the thought made his heart twist with a trapped animal's fright.

He sat up and noticed clean clothing laid across the end of the bed. He rose and washed in the small utile room off the bedroom, and dressed. It was clumsy work, with one arm wrapped in white, stiff—not cloth, but something woven.

The routine helped clear his mind. He became conscious of his incredible luck in the blur of yesterday's events. He had escaped the Shaull and their giant prison orbitcity and the slow death they called interrogation. Instead, he was safe in a secret mountain Keep among people he never knew existed.

The place looked like a restored temple-villa of the first immigrants from O'Nel-La, back before the Tidal Wars when the Northern Dominion, roughly half the United Continents, decided that their future looked brighter on Julle. They took their metallic technology and headed for richer mines. Julle was less than perfect, being farther from the ore-laden Tides, but it was free from Ecology Law.

The villa was old, must have been built before the exodus on to the Ringcity, belonged to some slaver noble; it fit their style.

The Cizrenhi had glazed the walls and pillars white, adding coverlets, rugs, and drapes in shades of russet and gold. Brace thought it austere, like a desert in the middle of an oasis.

There was a long-necked musical instrument on the wall above his bed. The other bed was either freshly made or never used. He wondered where Nyjehnn had slept; he'd left after seeing Brace to bed. Brace bent and stroked the pillow's day cover. Its quilted surface imparted a gentle female aura, weakened by time. The image of Cintha as he'd seen her in the library came to his mind. This was her bed, though she hadn't slept in it last night. He checked his bed; yes, Nyjehnn's. He was brushed by envy, an envy bred from long loneliness. The simple closeness this room shared made him feel so suddenly empty.

He realized he was little more than a string of chaotic events. Looking back, the years of his life seemed condensed into three crowded blocks of time. The first was his education at Yyerlos Biotech, a civilian primary school. He'd spent ten years there, active and absorbed in the concerns of surviving his childhood. Then, at thirteen, he'd gone off-planet, to Orbitbase Military Academy. The military had a way of filling the days of one's life so that you felt you were living two lives—one, an artificial practice at surviving rules, and the other, a life spent surviving death, lived in intense snatches of time labeled ALERT. But in all that long confusion of him, where was his existence? He neither loved nor hated the military; he'd not been given the choice. He was O'Nel and there was war, and that was the only meaning of his life.

At twenty he'd gone to the Storme Tides and entered flight training. Three years later, he'd been assigned a Starfish. The first thing his ship had taught him was the meaning of "lonely."

He'd lived his entire life surrounded by people every hour of every day, from barracks to mess hall, to classes, to duty stations, to flyball courts, and back to barracks. Drowning in people, but always alone. Not knowing what to call the emptiness until, in the synergism of Starfish flight, he experienced its opposite. Finally, there was another.

It was only semisentient, concerned mainly with sensing foreign intruders in his territory and finding energy. Yet it cooperated with him so closely that he felt himself one, in a symbiosis that expanded him beyond himself. He knew himself in flight as a powerful and free predator, at home in the fierce Tides, seeking out the enemy by stealth and speed, destroying the metal skins of their ships with his corrosive barbs.

Out of flight, too, he was something more, a unique being; not everyone had the control to pilot a Starfish. This new awareness of how exact the control of his own actions could be, gave him, finally, the sense that he wasn't just a military machine, but a human being with talents and powers and value above that provided by rank.

Now, with capture and the crash and rescue, he moved in another block of time, this one disassociated from every familiar reference he'd known. A disembodied voice from the distant Tides rang through his mind. "You are O'Nel," it reminded him. It echoed down the twisted alleys of his being and fell, drowned in the sunlit rug under his feet. What did O'Nel mean here, millions of kilometers from his ship and his purpose?

The morning's answer was silence, and it threatened to drown him as well. He bolted through the door to find Nyjehnn.

Brace crossed the ocher courtyard, glancing up at the strange-colored sun. Yann was small and wan where Reth, the primary star, was grand and golden. He felt cold here though it was the summer side of autumn. He strode under the balcony's shadow and entered an open doorway. The room inside was spacious and skylighted. It was an all-purpose living, dining, and kitchen area decorated with a jungle of plants. They hung from the rafters, along with large, light-filled globes; they grew in pots footing the tall east windows; and they cascaded down the pantry shelves in the kitchen. Brace felt a little more at home among the green.

There was a woven white grass rug on the stone floor and a simple trestlework dining table on his left. There was a tray of fruit and nutcakes laid out there with a ready place setting and a glass of what proved to be (when he tasted it) apple cider.

Brace pulled the bench under him, suddenly conscious that his last meal had been two days ago and he hadn't had much of an appetite for it. Now, he was ravenous. But he found he couldn't eat much. The silence of the room made him self-conscious, and after the first pangs had been satisfied, he rose and wandered back outside.

Turning right, he met a flight of stairs leading to the second-story balcony. As he mounted the steps, the clue of a rhythmic sound led him upward to an open door at the head of the stairs. He saw Cintha working at a large wooden floor loom. It was one of three looms in the neatly arranged workshop. There were also two spinning wheels, a wall hung with multicolored yarn skeins, and wide casement windows to the east and north.

Cintha sat in the bright weaving room wearing a long, green wist. With her waterfall hair braided down her back, she looked like an emerald in a platinum setting. Her beauty made Brace pause. The swinging rhythm of the weft beater stopped as he crossed the threshold.

Cintha turned and half rose from her bench. "What's wrong?" Concern drew her hand to the stiff, high-collared tabard over her heart.

"Nothing. I was looking for Nyjehnn."

"Oh, Brace." She sighed with relief. "I thought you were Khast and that something had . . ." She sat down again to hide her embarrassment.

"Do I resemble this . . . Khast that much?"

"I don't know. But you wear his clothes, and that fooled me." She placed her narrow shuttle on the woven warp. "Nyjehnn's out with the others. Come." She curled a finger and led him to the east windows. "Yes, they're still exercising." She offered him the view.

Brace looked down to the grass below. Nyjehnn, paired with a man in shoulder-length hair, were moving in exact unison. Both bare to the waist, they stepped out a pattern that looked part dance and part ritual combat. The two turned in sudden precision, like man and mirror image, and jumped high into back somersaults. They landed like loosed arrows, perfect to the second, and bowed to each other. Nyjehnn looked up and waved.

Brace waved back. "That must take a lot of practice."

"Not really." Cintha smiled. "One mind leads. Nyjehnn will be up in a minute. How's your arm?" She continued to stare out the window.

On a growing hunch, Brace interposed his hand between the view and her directionless gaze.

"My arm's fine, thank you. You can't see!"

Cintha turned to him. "No, not like you. But I see your form with my inner eyes. When Nyjehnn comes, he'll show me how you look. I will ask to borrow his sight. I often do."

"To do that?" He pointed to the loom.

"No. I can weave on my own. It's very much a tactile art. Come here." She sat on the bench again and ran her fingers across the cloth. "I can feel the tension, the selvages, the pattern of colors. This is brown; it feels warm and earthy. And this is rose, a different warmth, like that of bodies."

Brace became aware of the warmth in himself. Cintha was like no one he'd ever seen. She was a new wonder, but she was also familiar. Then he remembered why she didn't seem so impossible.

"You people remind me of an old O'Nel legend. It's said that long ago there were beings called Nel' A'Sheylii, half human, half angel. People who could travel without walking and talk without speaking. They were silver people who slept on clouds and danced on the wind. I never thought to meet a legend."

Cintha laughed with a clap of her slim hands. "Oh, how beautiful! Silver people on clouds and dancing with the wind." For a moment her eyes seemed less darkened. She tilted her head as if it were too heavy with memories. "It's been a long time." Her voice became husky. "Nyjehnn and I used to play flying—a mind trick we'd learned. But that was before coming Outside." She turned back to her loom.

"Were you blind before Outside?"

"Yes. A lightning storm. My best friend was dying and wanted to see me. I thought if I timed my jump . . . well, part of me was glad not to have sight then, not to see Chalie die. Hearing her was hard enough." She straightened. "He's coming."

Brace barely caught her words before Nyjehnn stepped out of the sunlight beside her. He had changed to cool white: fitted tans and a gauzy pullover shirt with beaded ties instead of a collar. He was barefoot, and his braided hair was damp.

"Good morning. Sleep well?"

"Yes, thank you." Brace was startled again by their striking twinlike resemblance. Not that Cintha was masculine or Nyjehnn feminine. Those simple polarities didn't apply here; Cintha's bodice was as flat as Nyjehnn's shirt, and his cheek as naturally smooth as hers. They were ageless in one sense, and at the same time pubescent. They reminded him of identical pale blossoms, one growing in sun and the other in shade.

Cintha took her brother's hand. "Brace has been telling me that I am a legend." She looked at Nyjehnn knowingly.

Brace, suddenly embarrassed, pretended to inspect the fine grain of the loom. He looked up to see Cintha's fawn eyes upon him. He started to smile, but her changing expression stopped him. It was a look of recognition and fear. It mounted as she stood and backed away.

"Let go, Nyjehnn!" She pleaded. "It's him—the one in my dream." She pulled away from her brother and vanished, leaving a stunned Nyjehnn and a bewildered Brace to stare at one another in the abrupt emptiness.

"Wait here," said Nyjehnn. "I'll be right back." He turned and was gone.

PETAL THE TWELFTH

Cintha knelt in the dim underground communatory. Only a faint radiance fell from a circle of sunballs netted in crystal near the ceiling. The four stone walls sparked with gems—the symbolized constellations of the Sacred Migration, the past and future history of the Cizrenhi Guardianship. There were twelve patterns measuring out the ponderous nomadic millennia, the orbital period of their star around the galactic heart, a nebulous blue-fire ball, Mornsyth, the sun of Cizren.

Nyjehnn settled close and comforted her trembling with an arm around her shoulders. But he didn't speak aloud, for in a way this room was their

Inside now, a tie to their real home, their "Place of Beginning." This haven was for the inner self and its speech of holy silence.

("Only a dream, Sister.")

Cintha denied his explanation with a shake of her head. She looked him straight in the eyes and forced upon his inner sight the nightmare which had haunted her for nearly a month. In the vision, he recognized a disheveled Brace standing over his own sprawled form, and blood on the stone in Brace's hand.

("Your blood!") Cintha emphasized fiercely.

Nyjehnn shrank from her certainty. Then leaned closer with silent disuasions, pushing them at her like a persistent flood surging against a virgin dike. Gentle reasonings, until finally she lowered her eyes.

The soft light haloed her hair with gold. ("Last night? You agreed he was a killer.") She reminded him of their talk after dinner.

("Had killed,") he corrected. ("And could again, with just cause.") He raised a hand at her foreseen objection. ("Yes. It makes no sense. But a difference exists between compulsive acts and temporary conditioning. Remember his place.")

Cintha sighed, her mind no calmer, but weary under the stress of the prophecy. ("Visions are a curse.")

("Never think that. It's a wise gift. I'll keep it in mind.") He touched her cheek.

Cintha took his hand, her dark eyes glittering. ("I'm so afraid. What I've seen cannot be set aside. If anything happens to you . . . I won't be able to go on. You're all I have.")

("Nothing will happen that we can't face. We've been through too much together not to know that.")

("Because we were together.")

("Trust me. I don't want to see you sad. I love you.") He gave her a quick hug and she clung to him a moment longer.

("I know. And I love you—too much. I can't help it. I almost lost you once.") She released him and sat back. She shook her head. ("Never again. I'll do anything within my power . . .")

Nyjehnn gave her the sign one makes to reassure crying children. ("Mother told me to take care of you. And I will.")

Cintha looked down. ("Ah, Mother.") She bloomed with memories of home and her imagery lapped into Nyjehnn like waves healing the trampled sand of a shore. There, in a softer sunlight, was their mother, Jenna, a stronger, wiser version of Cintha. She was turning from a council of friends, smiling at them warmly, turning back quickly to respond to a query. . . . Their father, Eathan, appeared, head bent in concentration over his seven-stringed lyrent. . . . It was the very one that now hung on the wall above Nyjehnn's bed. Mother again, walking in from her pampered garden, a basket of cumbers on her arm. . . .

Cintha sighed. ("She told me the same thing. 'Watch after your brother,' she said.") Her nostalgic smile vanished. ("Do you think she saw something?")

Nyjehnn considered. ("No. She wouldn't have let us come.")

("Or she would've come with us.")

("Yes. Even if it did mean revoking her Stewardship. No one would've touched Dh'exai land during the required two hundred siors. But suppose none of us came back?") He was reviewing what Jenna had presented to them when she'd explained her desire to stay home. She'd said, some liked to travel, and some liked to stay in one place, and thank the Lady for both.

Nyjehnn touched Cintha's knee. ("Are you all right now?")

("Better. I didn't sleep last night, did you?")

("No.") They hadn't slept apart since their father's death. At first it was for the constant care Nyjehnn had needed, then for his nightmares, and then simply because she felt more safe with him nearby during the dark nights. ("I'll move Brace to one of the spare rooms upstairs.") He stood and kissed the top of her head and left her to the prayer he knew she would pray.

She smiled after him through unshed tears.

Nyjehnn returned to the weaving room. Brace was sitting at Cintha's loom, admiring her work. He looked up.

"Is she all right?"

"Yes, don't worry." He brushed drying wisps of hair from his eyes. "She's fine."

Brace rose and crossed to the window. "She said she saw me in a dream. How can she dream about the future?" Silently he wondered what she'd seen that upset her so much. It upset him, too. "Isn't that impossible?"

"No," said Nyjehnn bluntly. "Not from our point of view."

"What do you mean, your point of view? Are you from the future?"

Nyjehnn was puzzled a moment as if the idea was new. "No. I meant that according to Nordawv physics, future, present, past," he shrugged, "it's all the same Now."

"I'm no physicist. I won't even pretend to understand." But he had to know the dream. "But what did she dream? Do you know?"

"Yes, but I'd rather not talk about it."

Brace persisted. "Why?"

"Because Cintha's visions have never been wrong."

"I gathered that." He waited.

Nyjehnn came and sat on the chest beside the window. "I pointed out to her that meanings can be misinterpreted."

"Okay. What does she think she saw."

Nyjehnn gazed out the window a long moment. "My death," he said at last.

The shock hung on Brace. "Not at my hands!" It was both a statement and a question pleading for negation.

Nyjehnn didn't turn from the window. "Yes."

Brace leaned closer, demanding his attention. "No! That's absurd. Not you." Their eyes met, and a recognition of the trust he had in himself flashed between them.

"I believe you," said Nyjehnn quietly.

"But you also believe her," he argued.

Nyjehnn looked out again. "Yes. I trust her gift."

Brace studied his boyish profile. "So, what do we do? Lock me up until I leave?"

Nyjehnn stared at him quizzically. "You say the strangest things. There are no locks here. We'll just go on, doing what needs done next, and next, and then. Which is what I should be doing now." He stood and smoothed his tans. "I'll be clearing a room for you at the end of the balcony, if you want to help."

He left and Brace continued to sit in the window, feeling like a timed bomb. He stared down at the roof of a steamy greenhouse, the lawn and the field beyond it and wondered what to do. Wait—that was all he could do, and hope Cintha was wrong.

With Nyjehnn gone, the silence folded its heavy cloak around Brace again. He knew now why it bothered him. Every cell of his being was accustomed to the familiar, comforting vibrations of his Orbitbase home, his ship, even the enemy Sprint. Now the loss of this "purring" let the silence in to press on him, body and soul. It gave him a fear that he was not only lost, but utterly abandoned, alone, and slowly being stripped of everything, even of his sense of himself that had sustained him during his capture by the Shaull.

He wondered how long he could stay here. These people of Cizren were mystifying and distant in a way that made him feel inadequate. There had come brief times when he'd felt the stir of friendship between Nyjehnn, Cintha, and himself, but then they turned those black-as-space eyes on him, chilling his heart. They were alien eyes that saw too much, and offered little of safety or familiarity. Eyes that only reminded him how much he was alone. Yes, Nyjehnn believed him, but he was still afraid of him; Brace could sense it. And now Cintha was afraid, too.

PETAL THE THIRTEENTH

Seyone was in Mazzad's apartments in the Hendar Summer Tower. They overlooked the continent of Altjia and the Altjiam Ocean. There was a tropical hurricane spinning slowly off the coast. Seyone lay across the divan in the sunken half of the gray-toned living room, watching the feathered thunderheads rotate below her in a white sprial on blue. She twisted a strand of her short black hair in the same direction, unconsciously.

The storm didn't look dangerous from up here. It didn't look real, but that's the way everything looked from the Ring. The vast scene below, shimmering between its convex horizons, might be a giant vidscreen. It took an act of will to convince herself of its reality.

She had lived her first fifteen years down there, traveling from pre-exodus ruin to ruin in a caravan of creaking wagons and travoises, scavenging and trading, dancing for food to the beat of the ever-present march drums. It was one long blur of heat and dust in her memory, a life that someone else had lived, on a world that was larger than this one, dangling at the end of her outstretched fingers. No, it wasn't real and neither was her itinerant past. It was a confused dream grown old and faded in the mind's telling, and now mostly forgiven—mostly.

Seyone sighed and sat up. The bell on her ankle jingled once. She had one regret, but he was dead, so she would carry her regret to her own grave, and there lie down beside him.

She still wore the red cape, though it was hours since Mazzad had sent her here to wait. Waiting was a slave's recreation. She had reset the climate controls, unpacked and stored the uniforms, and stocked the kitchen. She wasn't hungry; she'd been fed by the slaves in Grandarch Hendar's bakery while they'd prepared a tray for her owner and gossiped.

She hadn't much to exchange, living in the mazelike confines of a Vedette Starsprint for the last two years. It was a narrow existence in more ways than one; she felt that now, in the open planetlight of the City. From the bakers she'd learned that the Grandarch was dying and rumor said that he would leave everything to his niece, Mazzad. This didn't impress them with any hope for change; one Hendar was the same as any other, they'd told her. She agreed, noncommittally, because she hadn't given it much thought. In her mind, the Hendars and all other persons above slave rank were the adults in this world. The slaves were indentured children, purchased for life, sterilized and marked to insure their adolescent impotence. The more noncooperative were also silenced and drugged. The disobedient were killed. There were no prisons on the Ring; death was the punishment for any infraction of the law.

The Cencom screen beeped. Seyone left the cape on the divan. In a yellow silk caftan, she crossed to the gray carpeting and up to the dining level. She activated the monitor on the table. Mazzad's haggard face came into focus.

"I'm staying for my uncle's rites, then leaving immediately from there. Meet me on board my personal Wing with a fresh blue." She tugged uncomfortably at her collar braids. "I'd forgotten how much I hate dress whites." She held a card up to the screen for a moment, her fingers obscuring the ID codes. "Recognize this man? Good. Don't say his name aloud. I want you to contact him for me, *directly.*" She emphasized the last word. "Don't use my phone. Don't use a public phone. Tell him I want him and two top crews, and cleaned ships. He'll know what I mean. You know where to find him, Seyone?"

"Yes."

"Good. See to it." The screen went dark.

Where are we going? How long will we be gone? When will you be on board? Seyone turned off the monitor without the answers. Well, at least the waiting was over, for a while. She entered the bedroom to pack, again. Personal Wing, one uniform; obviously not a long trip. But Jessan Dalt, a medical staff shield officer as Second? That was odd. He lived and worked in the hospital tower. He'd been the Fleet's medical supervisor before their assignment to the Tides. A rare officer, one who spoke to Seyone as if she were a person who mattered, instead of a slave, a child.

She dropped the bags by the door and retrieved

her cape. She wondered if she should shut down the apartment, then decided against it, shouldered the bags, and locked the door behind her.

She rode down to the plaza level and crossed the wide squares of bright stone. It was midafternoon and pleasantly warm, and the vendors were busy with their ices and drinks. She waited while a class of kinders passed, marching in single file, their young faces serious and haughty. She wondered if they ever laughed. When, for that matter, was the last time she'd laughed? She shrugged and turned onto the main avenue. It was tree-lined, softening the reflected glare from the glassy towers. She passed a wealthy matron-type with a slave on a leash. The young man had blond hair and skin like purified honey. He was dressed in white and pretty, in a boyish way. Seyone's heart faltered a beat but recovered; it was only a disturbing likeness of Him. It didn't happen offen; there weren't many blond slaves. Besides, the poor thing was drugged. She could tell by his withdrawn preoccupation.

Seyone crossed an intersection and entered a public terminal. She flashed her ID bracelet, boarded a half-empty City-zone car, and consulted a map about the proper stop for the hospital. Altjia Summer Medical Center: it was three stops away.

She had Mazzad to thank that she could read. After purchase, she had been sent to school for one entire year. Seyone sat near the windows and put the bags beside her. A cadet across the aisle smiled at her and noted the bags. She recognized him from Mazzad's office and smiled politely in return. The car moved away from the station.

"Going back out already?" asked the cadet.

"Yes. I guess so." She settled to watch the avenue below. She didn't like talking to strangers.

The cadet crossed the aisle and sat behind her, leaning over the inside seat. He was sucking a mint.

"I'm just getting off duty," he said, scrubbing his dark cropped hair. "I heard Mazzad lost a ship today."

Seyone regarded him with a mixture of wonder and suspicion. One didn't tell slaves such things. His manner was so casual.

"I didn't know that," she replied. Now she knew why she was on her way to see Jessan Dalt.

"It crashed on the surface." He nodded toward the northern hemisphere, hazy and blue on their left.

Seyone's hand tightened on the straps she still held. We're going down there? The thought troubled her. She'd made her peace with the past, but she wanted the past to stay the past. The car entered the medical tower and slowed. She sat forward.

"I get off here." She stood.

The cadet reached for the bags. "Let me help you with those. They look too heavy for a little thing like you."

"No." She shouldered the straps. "They're not. Excuse me." His offer reminded her of Mazzad's warnings: don't say the name, don't use the phone; she wanted secrecy. Seyone hurried off, wishing for once in her life to be lost in a crowd. But there was no crowd in the hospital lobby, and the cadet was following her.

She took an up bubble and got off at the administration level. The clerk at the outer desk directed her to the military tower next door. She could use the skybridge at the end of the hall. Seyone crossed, looking behind her. There was no sign of him.

In the lobby, she examined the public register and found the name and ward number. Slaves weren't allowed to file a private pager, so she went up another four levels and stated her request to convey a message on behalf of Mazzad Hendar. She was told that Officer Dalt was in emergency surgery.

She would wait. She was good at waiting. Sometimes it felt her entire life was one long wait. Her mind asked, waiting for what? Her heart answered, I'll know when it comes.

PETAL THE FOURTEENTH

Seyone was shaken from sleep by a determined hand on her shoulder. She looked up at Jessan Dalt, still dressed in his greens. "You have a message from Mazzad?" He sat in the chair beside her. He had a fair, open face and curly black hair graying over his ears, and blue eyes with a delta of wrinkles at their corners. "How long've you been waiting?" He touched her wrist as if taking her pulse.

She straightened. "I don't know." She looked out the long windows; it was night. "Oh, no. I'll be punished."

"Calm down. I'll accept responsibility. What's the message?"

"She directed me to tell you in person that she wants you, two top crews, and cleaned ships. She said you'd know what she meant."

Dalt nodded seriously. "Yes, I know what she wants."

"Also, I think it's important . . ." began Seyone, not sure if she was right to mention it at all.

"Yes, what?"

"I think I was followed here."

Dalt became guarded. "What did he look like?"

"A cadet, short brown hair, tight eyes. He talked to me on the Tube and tried to carry my bags here. He told me Mazzad lost a ship on the surface. Is that true?"

Dalt took her bags and pulled her up. "Let's find out."

They hurried through the wards to a private lobby and took an express down to his apartment in the core. He stopped long enough to grab a packed carry-on.

"I'll change on board," he explained.

With a shield officer's ID, they rode the Cencom underrail to the Hendar Tower, both on the alert for a cadet or anyone else going their way at their speed. Dalt's calm effectiveness at moving around the city made Seyone feel safe. They rode alone in an outer bubble up to the Space Docks, and watched the City's avenues grow small in a canyon of blazing towers.

They arrived at the cavernous hangar deck with its chevron-lit space chutes. Mazzad's Wing-class Sprint waited on the pad. Another Wing sat nearby. They boarded the ramp to Mazzad's Wing, passing a lance officer on his way down.

"Is the Pack Reeve on board?" asked Dalt.

He saluted. "No, Shield. Not yet."

Dalt smiled at Seyone, a flash of even teeth. "If

we're fast, we can get an hour's work done in fifteen minutes. If you would help," he added.

"I don't know anything about ships."

"You can do this."

Dalt led her into medbay and dropped the bags. From a wall-cabinet pouch, he took a transparent card and showed it to her.

"I want you to take this into every cabin on the ship. Check the area like this." He circled the medbay, waving the card in wide, slow arcs. "If it starts to vibrate, call me." He gave her the card. "I'll be on the bridge." He paused in the hatchway. "Oh, and check the lifeboat, too."

Seyone walked throughout the ship. Once she thought she felt a tingling, then realized she'd been holding the card too tightly. She relaxed her grip and checked the galley again. It was quiet. She went down the aft ramp, opened the double hatches, and entered the lifeboat shuttle. It was dark except for the green exit lamp and the hatchway light behind her.

As she stepped toward the cabin lights, crushing arms pliered her from behind. The card went flying. Her mouth was smothered by a hard hand. She smelled mint, and a male voice hissed in her ear, "Don't make a sound."

Seyone was lifted off her feet. She heard the shuttle hatch close; then she was shoved into a passenger seat and held down.

"I'm used to the dark," said the cadet. "You're the slave . . . Seyone. I have a gun, Seyone. Don't make me use it on you."

Her eyes were adjusting to the darkness, and she could see he was telling the truth. Her mind was blank with shock.

"I was sent for your Hendar master." He let up on her and sat in the facing seat. "Haven't you wanted her dead? Haven't you wanted the whole rotted dynasty dead and damned? Don't you want your freedom?"

"Who . . . who?" Seyone stammered. She was very cold.

"No, I'm not a cadet. I'm a keftain—World Refugee Corps. My name's not important, just the mission. Don't move." He reached behind him and turned up the volume on an in-ship channel. Mazzad's crisp voice came from the speakers.

"Anything turn up?"

"No, not yet." It was Dalt's voice. "Who would sabotage your ships? That's not the way it's done."

"You're an expert on assassinations now?"

In the shuttle, the keftain sat facing Seyone, listening and watching her listen. "She always sounds like she's talking to morons. Ever notice that?"

Dalt's voice said, "You really think it's the family? There's so few of you left. Why would they risk the dynasty?"

The keftain nodded. "Dalt's smart. Is he armed?"

Seyone shook her head.

The voice of Mazzad answered, "Maybe it's too small a bone for too many dogs." A rustle of paper. "How soon to launch?"

The keftain closed the channel, stood, and pulled Seyone close. "It's just too many dogs. Here, keep this for me." He pulled off his rank ring and gave it to her. "Let's go. Don't give any alarm. I don't want to kill you." He held her in front of him and opened the hatch.

On the bridge, Dalt and Mazzad were huddled over the navigation console. The tracer's screen was lit with a continent outline. Mazzad was entering coordinates.

"Twenty-seven north, sixty-three west." A light blinked on the screen.

"A scant this side of nowhere," observed Dalt.

Mazzad unsnapped her jacket and rubbed her eyes.

"Don't move, Pack Reeve!" The cadet stood in the hatchway, using Seyone as a shield.

Mazzad saw his gun and kept her hands raised. She looked at Dalt. They both looked at the security button. Mazzad laughed at the assassin. "Well, twice in one night. What makes me such a popular target?"

Three things happened simultaneously: Mazzad dove to her right, behind the weapons pit; Dalt hit the security button and threw himself to the deck; and the assassin pushed Seyone and fired at Mazzad. The weapons pit exploded in showering sparks and smoke. He stepped over Seyone and fired again. Dalt launched himself at the gunman, who knocked him aside. Mazzad fired in that second of distraction, and he went down.

Dalt got to his feet, bent over the unconscious man, and felt for a pulse at his neck.

"He's still alive." There was a laser burn on his left side.

"Good." Mazzad came over, the left sleeve of her dress uniform smoking and a red stain spreading.

Two security officers came onto the bridge, weapons ready.

Mazzad pointed to the assassin. "Put him in my cage."

They pulled the man down the passageway. Dalt knelt beside Seyone, who lay shivering and staring, vacant-eyed.

"She's in shock." He looked up. "You'll be the same if I don't take care of that."

Mazzad looked at her arm. "Later. I want some answers before he dies." She gestured at Seyone. "Give her a sedative and put her to bed. She'll be all right." She left the bridge and met a crewman coming on board. "Find an ordinance man. The weapons pit needs repair. Now!" He left on the run.

She entered the interrogation lounge, across from the bridge. It was an area of decadence and cruelty and said so in plush observer's chairs and bright computerized instruments. A glass-enclosed platform filled the center of the cabin. Behind it, on the outer bulkhead, hung the computer panel flanked by frescoed scenes of freefall cities, earlier evolutions of the Ring. The assassin sat propped inside the cage. He was conscious.

Mazzad holstered her weapon and stood looking down at him. "Why don't we make this quick. Who hired you?"

The man smiled and shook his head like he'd heard one too many bad jokes. "Go to hell."

"You first." She turned and made herself comfortable in one of the chairs. She pointed to the computer panel and said to one of the guards, "Hand me the remote." He complied.

She activated the cage at sone one. The man inside shuddered and struggled to sit upright, away from the glass.

"One name." She waited a moment, then pressed sone three. The captive grunted and held his ears, rocking with pain. Sone five and the man wailed and threw himself against the glass. She cut the power and stood up. "Who hired you?"

He lay on the platform, his right hand fumbling at his boot. "Eki-ji," he whispered. He drew a knife and slit his throat.

Mazzad swore and kicked the base of the cage. She threw the remote at the guards. "You didn't search him? You stupid slugs! Every soldier carries two deaths. One for his success"—she pulled her own knife from its boot sheath—"and one for his failure—Eki-ji code. Where in the hell did you train?" She sat down abruptly, dizzy. "Get it out of here." They hurried to obey.

Dalt was standing in the hatchway with a compress and antiseptic spray.

She sheathed her knife and removed her jacket. "Are the crew aboard yet? I've had enough delays."

"Yes." He sprayed her arm and bandaged it.

"Good. And get into a uniform. You look like hell."

"So do you."

PETAL THE FIFTEENTH

The old Nordawvese settled beside Nyjehnn on the big floor pillows in his sparse room next to the library. He imposed his owlish eyes admonishingly.

"You're not concentrating. You still look tired. Are you up to doing this now?"

"I don't think putting it off will help." He stroked the sunball cradled in his lap. "I'll try again."

"Very well." Marce smoothed his long mustache and folded his four hands atop themselves, his habitual meditation pose. He slowed the intonations.

"Relax. . . .

"Release. . . .

"Reclaim. . . .

"Remember. . . .

"Concentrate the light."

Nyjehnn closed his eyes and relaxed the tension in his shoulders and neck. He released his mind from its daily thoughts to reclaim his overself in this moment and fasten to the true intent of his life. He searched and found the place in his mind where the remembering of this ritual was stored. Marce's rumbling chant echoed it through him like notes creating music. He sent his conscious will, with the light, into the sunball.

Marce pulled him deeper.

"You are light within light.

"Her golden universe embraces.

"Let brightness define each sun.

"Reach . . . search . . . find.

"Peace without time is now . . . now."

"I am All. I am Nothing," whispered Nyjehnn. He let go of his breath, as incense releases fragrance, in a long, drifting sigh.

Marce nodded with approval and relief as Nyjehnn entered the trance pattern used to integrate consciousness beyond ego, an essential for communication between the Guardians strewn across the vibrant void of space.

"Qi'nin, qi'nin." Nyjehnn's soft voice faded, then became a duple. "O'Inin, o'Inin." The two-voice harmony confirmed the Starlink. The rest of the conversation flashed above the silence of the solar winds, swirling between inner and outer sun.

Marce sat back in meditation. Part of him listened for Nyjehnn's return to breathing, the signal that the link was over. Another part he focused on the mat under his knees and the line of Nyjehnn's shadow lying on the weave. He watched his ordered thoughts, now amused, now with interest, pursuing delicate tendrils of present and past. There were parts of him in many things, places, and people. He had the habit now after these centuries of working for the Nordawv Galactic Archives.

He'd had an illustrious tenure, gone on to field work, and now all his parts revolved around the greatest discovery of his career: the nomadic Cizrenhi. Proof of their existence had been the central passion of his life, and it was both boon and curse that his desire had been fulfilled. For now, in his understanding of their powers and vulnerabilities, in his devotion to their protection, he was their most eminent authority, but he was also, inescapably, their devotee. His many parts—teacher, historian, scientist, and philosopher—were in their service. In exchange, they gave him (Nyjehnn's family foremost) the single most essential element to a Nordawvese: purpose.

Marce had been with the Dh'exai family from his first chance meeting with Thaj, Nyjehnn's grandfather, over a thousand years ago. It was on the steps of an abandoned temple on the planet Suaad. Marce had been on a research side trip, a last-minute sort of thing. The Cizrenhi man had appeared out of thin air, startling him.

He hadn't seen Marce at first; he was intent on the Aixerthon script carved into the foundation stones. Curious, Marce had approached him. When his shadow touched the relief, the Cizrenhi whirled, quite shocked, and said, "How did you do that?"

Only his lips hadn't moved, yet Marce had heard the Suaadian words clearly in his mind. Shocked himself, he blurted, "What?" It was a stupid thing to say, but he sensed he'd frightened the other man badly, and wanted to assure him of his innocent intentions.

The Cizrenhi wore an ankle-length robe, rather like Marce's, and had long, black hair worn in a thick braid. He was humanoid and seemed a mature specimen, though he had no facial hair.

He stood and said, "You could've killed me and I'd not have known until too late. How were you able to approach without my sensing you?" Again, his lips hadn't moved.

Marce remembered becoming excited. At first he'd thought it was because this might be the race he'd been searching for these past six thousand years or so, following a trail from system to system of mythos, warding signs, and archetype legends.

He apologized to the wary man, introduced himself, and explained his curiosity.

"I am called Thaj," said the other. They talked under the red sun until, quite suddenly, Marce passed out. When he awoke, a few minutes later, Thaj apologized in turn, and told him how to mirror his mind, how to use his own energy to reflect a telepath's thoughts so that the inspeech didn't excite the brain, causing it to snap off like an overloaded circuit.

Telepathic, telekinetic—this was indeed the dimorphic race of star nomads he'd been tracking. Marce explained his research, and the dream behind it: to found a network for the purpose of education and communication, a step toward his vision of a fully conscious galaxy on the material level that would benefit all its inhabitants.

Thaj invited him to his tents, huge flat sails anchored to the warm dunes. They were spacious and made comfortable with many rugs and large pillows. There he'd met Thaj's young son, Eathan, and learned of their stellar explorations. He, in turn, had explained his idea. The Cizrenhi were fascinated with Marce's vision, and from that day Marce had been ensnared by them, willingly. He'd returned with them to Cizren when Migration had called them back.

Thaj and Eathan assured him that the Cizrenhi were ready for a new era. Before Marce, their migrations had been only playful, meaningless wanderings. True, they'd learned much, but what good was all the knowledge? They'd begun to question their reasons for coming Outside. To what end could they put all the exploration and information? Marce gave them a reason to stay Outside. He took an Alliance proposal back to Nordawv.

If the people of Cizren had had any sense of a nobility, the Dh'exai would be the royal family. It had been Nyjehnn's mother's line who had discovered Outside and started the Sacred Migrations. The closest thing to a term of status on Cizren was the term "Kathen," which translated as "honored one" and "friend." This had been the Dh'exai title for generations. They lived in a sprawling interconnected village built of glass and dark redwood. Marce felt at home in its civilized use of solar and thermal energy. The families living on Dh'exai land were curious but friendly.

He had attended the birth of Nyjehnn Kathen Dh'exai, and had accepted Jenna's request that he educate her firstborn. Cizrenhi children were raised in-Keep for their first five years, then sent to the Sant'kye Temple for five years of training in physical discipline. After that she would send Nyjehnn to him.

Marce admired the Sant'kye discipline, part sport and part dance, but the Cizrenhi were unaware that other races used a darker version for attack and defense. These peaceful beings had no word for war and no word for enemy; the lack of these two lingual concepts told everything about their culture.

Nor had they a word for stranger, until Marce. Their world was completely homogeneous in language and customs. Marce was the first Outsider to live among them. With the intragalactic Nordawv Archives behind him, he could teach them much.

During his last visit, he had sat watching Thaj deep-trance and speak with the Keeps throughout Cizren, planning the first Alliance dispersal. It would be the seventh Migration. It was to be the last one for Thaj. The memory brought him back to now.

Thaj, Eathan, and now, Nyjehnn; they were the facets of one gem. But there was a flaw in the gem and it worried him. Maybe it was a flaw in all Cizrenhi. He didn't know yet. The nomadic Dh'exai were courageous; they had to be to leave Cizren in what amounted to a form of death, but there was in them also a reckless compulsion for sacrifice. Thaj had died from the stones of a fanatic, trying to save the sanity of a young priest. Eathan had died from the hate of a friend, trying to reconcile his trust. He feared for Nyjehnn the same fate.

The shadow on the mat became Nyjehnn's dark twin, that part of him where he'd shut up the tragedies, but not without great cost. Nyjehnn had come Outside full of idealistic dreams, but in confronting death, they had died a little. With his own near-fatal brush, they had disappeared completely. All that remained was duty, attended to, Marce suspected, with an increasingly routine indifference. There were signs.

Marce studied Nyjehnn's iconic profile. It grieved him that there seemed not a thing he could do to bring back the child-hearted boy he had delighted in so much. He missed his catlike curiosity, his insatiable inquisitiveness about anything and everything in the vast universe. The perfect pupil was still there, but the exuberant pursuit of knowledge for the pure love of it was eclipsed. This saddened Marce, for he loved to teach, and Nyjehnn had his grandfather's remarkable mind.

He wished—not for the first time—that there was some way he could convince the boy to claim his right to be free of the past. In these last few years he had watched the young Dh'exai deepening toward a Cizrenhi mystic, more and more a reluctant creature of the world. He felt if it weren't for his duty to the Guardianship and loyalty to his sister, Nyjehnn would've let go of living. Even now, perhaps, his hold on it was only one of temporary agreement.

He recalled their last study session. He had tested Nyjehnn with an obscure riddle gleaned from an ancient Aixerthon codex.

> There was once a seer who dreamed a vision of his own imminent death. The cruel manner of it left him sick with horror. Upon awakening, he poisoned himself quietly to escape the vision. Now tell me, from whence came his death?

Nyjehnn had eyed him with good-natured suspicion but gave it serious thought for a full three minutes. "Time," he said finally, "was the slayer."

The answer hadn't matched any of the three recorded by some long-dead priest at the bottom of the brittle manuscript, so Marce had asked him to explain.

"I rejected the superficial causes: fear, pride, ignorance." He counted off the three. "Time is master of them all."

It had encouraged Marce that Nyjehnn was aware of this. Time was the answer he would have given. Time was the breath of the universe. And he, with the life span of a star, could afford time to answer every mystery and test of life. But what of Nyjehnn, whose years would number only half a century, if he chose to live them out? Marce took his mentorship seriously. The Cizrenhi, with their innocent ethics, needed his experience, their psychic genius needed his protection. Besides, they were his children and he adored them.

Nyjehnn's breath returned in a gasp. His eyes were open but unfocused. Marce moved expertly to hold him upright, slapping him lightly to help him concentrate on his body, and rubbing his hands to restore full circulation.

Nyjehnn focused on him and nodded. "Thanks." He clutched at one of Marce's upper hands. "Aunt Morthena—her Keep, O'Nel-La—it's true, the inner system is boiling in war. The tension there is unbelievable. I don't know how she manages." He shook his head. "She says Migration is her one sustaining hope."

"What about Brace?"

Nyjehnn smoothed back his hair. "He was right. Resources can't be diverted to rescue one pilot. Morthena says to let him stay. He's better off here."

"That must be his decision," reminded Marce.

"I know." He handed Marce the dimming sunball. "But he won't choose to stay."

"What makes you think that?"

"Just a feeling." He stood and stretched.

Marce shuffled to the wall, rose off his lower hands and placed the sunball back in its bracket.

"Well," he grunted. "When he decides to leave, you've still no transportation."

Nyjehnn waited at the door. "I know. I'll link with Deun Keep in the next system, send a thought out-system maybe, for a free merchant or a private shuttle."

"Maybe contact the—?"

"No," he interrupted. "I won't go to a Refugee. Neutral or not, I promised—no Shaull. How can you ask me that?"

"They're not all barbarians. They hate the City and the leeches who built it as much as Brace does.

They might be willing to suspend their neutrality long enough to help." He took an outer robe from his clothing chest and shook it unfolded.

"How would you know this?" Nyjehnn helped him into it.

"How is it that you do not?"

"You know how I feel about touching the tribes."

The Nordawvese plodded past him and out into the courtyard. The afternoon sun was falling into evening gold. Nyjehnn came into step and Marce said to him.

"Think about it being time to set aside feelings for the sake of the O'Nel boy."

Nyjehnn pocketed his hands and said nothing.

PETAL THE SIXTEENTH

The doors of the Common room were open front and back, and trusting birds fluttered in for their share of evening table crumbs. Around the table, where Nyjehnn sat at the head, were Marce, Brace, Willa, Khast, and LeAnn. Cintha had pleaded more time to meditate. Marce was in good spirits, but the rest were subdued and polite, the way people tend to be when strangers share their table. The room was filled with the setting sun.

Brace turned from feeding the birds and said to Marce, "Excuse me, sir. You're obviously not Cizrenhi. Are you stranded here, too?"

Marce chuckled deep in his old throat. "So some have said, young man. Also, some have said 'exiled,' and some, 'hiding.' " He shrugged his upper shoulders. "But I am here because this is where I chose to be. Have you heard of the Nordawv?"

"No, not before yesterday. Nyjehnn mentioned some kind of alliance between your races." Willa passed him the salad.

"Sponsorship would be a better definition. We provide for their living on the Outside while they maintain our network. Why are you here?"

Brace filled his bowl with greens. "Didn't Nyjehnn tell you? Sheer luck, as far as I'm concerned. This place is like a miracle. I should be dead." He gave the salad to Marce, who gave it to Nyjehnn, who handed it to LeAnn. She took a helping.

"Yes, the accident," continued Marce. "You consider it a fortunate event, then?" He poured himself a cup of tea.

Brace grew quiet. "For me, yes. Of course."

"And the pilot?" Marce and the Cizrenhi waited. It made Brace uncomfortable. He felt he was being tested.

"He was Shaull."

Their careful expressions didn't change.

"What is it? You want me to say I'm sorry he's dead? Forget it. I'm not sorry there's one less Shaull in the war."

Marce sipped his tea, thawing the mood. "Just a little 'seeing through your eyes.' No harm intended. Some bread?" He held the basket for Brace. The others returned to their meal.

Brace took a roll. "And what did you see?"

Nyjehnn picked a leaf from the salad bowl and said, "A man who sees two sides of a leaf, but not the whole plant." He paused as if someone had tapped him on the shoulder. "Oh."

Marce combed his wispy mustache with one finger. "Very good, Nyjehnn. So what will you do?"

"If it comes to that road, I'll consider it," Nyjehnn said.

"What's going on?" asked Brace.

"Marce was instructing me about choices. He never tires of these little tricks. He was also saying there's no such thing as chance."

"I disagree. I live by chance all the time." He buttered and ate a piece of roll.

Marce said, "Sheer luck, I believe."

"Right. Living's a fool's gamble. The rewards are few; the risks can be fatal," he shook his head, "but we come anyway."

The young woman sitting across from him pushed away her plate and glanced at Khast, her husband, next to her. He sat with an air of deliberate avoidance, circling the rim of his teacup with a calloused finger. LeAnn gathered her courage.

"What do you mean, 'we come anyway,' Mr. . . . ?"

"TelRden," supplied Brace. "I haven't had time to ponder that question much less answer it. If I knew, I probably wouldn't be here."

Khast said, "I wish you weren't." He stood to leave.

"Sit down," ordered Nyjehnn. Khast hesitated but obeyed.

Brace dropped his chopsticks. "I did not choose to be here!" He stepped away from the bench and strode out the back door, scattering birds. Nyjehnn watched him disappear among the tall corn of the garden, heading toward the stream at the foothills behind the Keep.

Willa stacked some plates. "That was very rude, Khast." She went into the kitchen. LeAnn followed with more dishes.

"Sorry, Nyjehnn," mumbled the young botanist.

"It's all right. I know how hard this is on you and LeAnn. It's uncomfortable for us all to have an Outside among us. But it's what we're here for. If we're not going to do the work, we might as well go home."

Khast looked at the nonjudgmental face of the Nordawv. "Maybe that's not such a bad idea."

Nyjehnn wasn't surprised, nor could he condemn him. The idea had been across his own mind more than once. "Does LeAnn feel that way, too?"

"I don't know. She doesn't talk about it. Besides, we're pledged to stay, aren't we?"

"A pledge to my father, not to me."

"A promise to a First, Nyjehnn. As far as I'm concerned, that's you now, with or without ceremony."

Nyjehnn was touched by his sincerity. "I'm sorry I yelled at you." He blamed his alarming fatigue.

Khast shrugged. "I guess I'll go after him." He nodded toward the back field. "It's almost sundown."

"No, I'll go," said Nyjehnn. He stood and squeezed Khast's shoulder and went out.

Through the garden and meadow, crossing a dry canal they had made for irrigation, Brace's trail veered left, upstream and under the trees. Nyjehnn jumped to the distant shade and stood listening to the sounds of Brace's passing drift back from the cool darkness. He followed the sounds, his mind still on Khast. A sensitive man and private much of the time, Khast honored him by naming him First. A little thing, but it renewed Nyjehnn's confidence. A minute later, he came out into a small, wildflowered clearing. Brace was sitting on the stream's grassy bank, his back to the low sun.

Nyjehnn came beside him. "Why did you run?"

Brace stayed seated, staring into the swift crystal water.

"You're all scared, except Marce." He looked up. "Even you. Why are you afraid of me? Is it because of Cintha?"

Nyjehnn sighed. "No, and it's not you, either. It's where you're from."

"O'Nel-La? I don't understand."

Nyjehnn sank down, crossing his feet. "I don't mean a location. I'm talking about an experience. You fell down on us from a 'place' called war. The effect it's had on you affects us. As I said last night, war is unknown among the Cizrenhi. Here, Outside, we haven't learned to accept it. We can't."

"How long have you been Outside?"

"Since my grandmother's mother, Nyath; generations now. There was a time when we didn't know what fear was, didn't know it even existed."

"You were fortunate. My people have been fighting in fear for over three hundred years."

"Ah, then," Nyjehnn said casually, "long enough to realize the futility of fighting."

Brace sat in shocked silence, not knowing what to answer. The words hit deep, piercing afresh a wound he thought he'd closed forever on the day he entered the Service. A hurt he thought well bandaged with tradition and logic to keep from bleeding half his soul away.

Nyjehnn yawned and stretched out on his stomach, resting his chin on his arm. "I'm sorry if I upset you."

"I'm not upset," lied Brace. "You echo my own beliefs. But I can't choose them anymore. I had to bury my rebellion in the graves of my family. I don't belong to myself. I won't until the war's over."

Nyjehnn was silent.

"I know, suppose it's never over. That's one thing that scares me; it's become a way of life for us. You must know a little of what that's like—living here under the hem of the City." He rubbed the back of his neck absently and looked down at Nyjehnn. He was asleep.

Brace succumbed to a wry chuckle. "Well, maybe you don't." He lifted Nyjehnn's thick braid off the ground and laid it across his back. He picked out a piece of clinging dry grass, then pulled a clean stalk nearby to chew. In sleep or awake, with their patient eyes and white-wheat hair, they had that transparent innocence of children that made Brace feel older than his twenty-six years.

He recalled the way they'd looked at him around the table, guileless as second-level kinders waiting for the teacher to finish reading them the story. No, not quite that naive; they'd known what Marce was doing. They hadn't been surprised at the story's ending. His answer was the expected one. Somehow, a myriad of messages had been conveyed in those brief moments: Marce told the Cizrenhi, "Yes, you're right to mistrust him. He's like all the others you've met." Nyjehnn had told Brace, "O'Nel, Shaull—you're all one." (Maybe it was once true, but not anymore.) Then Marce had told Nyjehnn he had more choices than he thought, and Nyjehnn claimed Marce had told everyone that chance was an illusion. That's where the old ape was wrong.

Chance was a fact of his short life. His late friend, Ril, would agree with him. Put two fliers in combat: one dies and one lives, and that's chance, right? Right. What else could it be? He sighed and turned to the afterglow of the sun in the west.

As twilight came in blue-violet, Cintha and Marce emerged from the trees. The girl's left hand rested on the Nordawv's stooped shoulders. She stared a steady and frightened accusation at Brace.

He got to his feet, raising his hands. "I didn't touch him. I was just thinking of coming for help."

He stepped back for Marce. The Nordawv took Nyjehnn's delicate wrist in a large hand.

Cintha stood hugging her arms. "Marce?"

Marce rolled Nyjehnn gently to his back. He tested his cheek and forehead.

"He's not just sleeping, is he?" asked Brace.

Marce ignored him. "Temperature and pulse very low. But not irreversible yet. I think we're in time." He gathered Nyjehnn into his arms easily and headed back. "He's much too light."

Cintha followed. "I know, I should've seen it coming. He's ignored food these past three days." She turned to Brace walking beside her. "Would you guide me, please?"

"Of course." He clasped her arm with his good hand. "What's wrong with him?"

She answered reluctantly. "He's going into hibernation. It's natural in winter, but sometimes if we become sick or very tired, it can overtake us anytime during the year. It happened once before when . . ." She changed the subject. "We must seem very unfriendly." She sounded much more at ease with him.

He steered her around a tree. "Nyjehnn was just explaining about that."

She gave him a puzzled frown. "He told you?"

"Something about me being a specter of war at a private party."

Brace was rewarded with a grim smile. "He didn't tell you. I didn't think he would. Even we don't talk about it."

"About what?"

"When we first came here, we lived in another Keep, farther south. There were many more of us, and my father, our father, was the First. We were very happy then."

He could barely discern her face in the forest darkness, but it sounded like there were waiting tears between the words.

They came out into the open field. Ahead, Marce was mounting the back steps of the Keep. He and his limp burden were outlined in the gold light spilling from the tall windows and doors.

"You don't have to tell me this," said Brace.

"It's all right. I want you to understand about us. It's not your fault." She held her braid with her free hand, her head down. "Anyway, a clan of traders camped near our Keep. Father decided we could learn from them and maybe trade our cloth and pottery. We made some friends. One young woman came often. I taught her to weave. We became very close, and she confided to me that she had fallen in love with Nyjehnn, but that it was impossible because he was not of her tribe. Well, it turned out not to matter. One day, slavers from the City descended on the trader camp, killing many and taking more. We never found out what happened to her."

They were on the lawn and came to the back steps. "Can we sit here for a while?"

"Sure," agreed Brace. He sat beside her.

"If I go in now, I'll just be in Willa's way. He's in the best of hands." Cintha curled her braid in her lap. "Anyway, Nyjehnn must've felt something for her; he was very sad that night and went for a long walk." She paused for a breath. "So he wasn't there when the men of the camp attacked." Her voice dropped to a whisper. "To this day I can't understand it. We were friends. They came to our chants.

"So many of us were killed. Noal, the master weaver, hid me in the Communatory and went back up for his mother. I never saw either of them again—alive. Lita, Khast's daughter, was strangled. Father died, too. It was winter, you see."

She was silent for a moment to regain her

composure. "I remember waiting in the dark, sending warnings to Nyjehnn—don't come, don't come back." There was a catch in her voice suddenly. "Oh, Nyjehnn, all the nights I prayed for you to come Outside because I missed you, and that night I prayed for you to stay away, but you didn't hear.

"That was the longest night of my life. I didn't care if I ever saw another Sunning."

She hugged herself. "Marce ventured out in the morning to gather the dead. He found Nyjehnn. He had been tied to the Keep gate." Cintha broke into full tears and leaned against Brace.

He put his arm around her. "I understand. Don't go on."

She tugged away and wiped her face. She looked straight at him, and he shivered with the thought that she could see the recognition of horror in his eyes. She took a breath. "They had beaten him near to death and cut off his hair, and it's my fault, all his pain. If I hadn't selfishly convinced him to come early, he would've been safe on Cizren."

Cintha stared blindly into the moonless night. "Nyjehnn couldn't speak for a year afterwards. It's been hard for him, for all of us, relocating, rebuilding, trying to heal our lives."

"Why did you stay?" Brace felt a confusion of emotions: sadness, helplessness, admiration, mixed with a fear that he was falling in love with Cintha and he must not.

"It's our duty to stay. Nyjehnn still has his honor."

Brace looked at Cintha and tried to say it as gently as possible. "So now, you're afraid I'll succeed where the traders failed."

She held her breath to hold back the tears.

"I won't hurt him. I promise you, Cintha. He saved my life."

"Could I be alone, please?" She laid her temple to her knees and closed her eyes.

"I'd like to stay."

She gave no answer so Brace stayed and waited with her. It was a warm night for autumn; tree frogs and crickets were talking in the forest. Brace listened, thinking of home and the dances they used to hold on nights like this in the park. He saw his parents dancing, happy.

"What are you thinking?" asked Cintha. Her eyes were still closed.

Brace sat twisting his fingers. "My parents are dead, too."

"Oh, I'm sorry." She sat up. "But that's not what was in your mind."

Brace laughed once. "I forgot. Living in a nest of telepaths, I'd better watch what I think."

"We don't intrude. But you were very open just now. I got a glimpse of people dancing among trees under the stars."

He nodded. "Twice a year we have gatherings. A whole community of families comes together to eat and sing and dance all night. We don't celebrate any special event, just the being together."

"It sounds wonderful. We have a festival like that. It's called Valendon, but it's never night on Cizren."

"Never?" The house lights dimmed behind him. He turned and saw LeAnn subracting light from the sunballs. "Then when do you sleep?"

"We never had the need for sleep until coming Outside. It's so dark out here." She looked up at the sky as if she were feeling the blackness with her face.

"I hate the dark," she whispered. "At least we have light in our dreams."

PETAL THE SEVENTEENTH

Nyjehnn was a dream of light moving toward expression. Just as there would be sound that flies beyond its barrier, singing messages unheard by any listening ear, bound for some unknown angel's hearing, there would be light, as yet unfolded, winging beyond its perceived limits, bearing a message that flies too swift for any seeing eye, traveling at the speed of thought.

This message knew its content, and it knew its destination, and in the dream it lived, again, its journey to Outside. That which would be Nyjehnn announced himself from his home world Cizren. Out he came, from its orbit around a blue-fire sun, out from the crowded stars of the center, out beyond the dark womb-ring that surrounded the galactic core, ten thousand light-years out in no time measured on any causal wheel.

He flew in disincarnate bliss, plunging unseen past starry veils and auroral clouds, past hurricanes of darkness, diving too swiftly for the sucking lips of gravity. He sailed further, past the star storms, with the ethereal solar waves crashing playfully through his buoyant soul. He fell unfettered from sun to sun, and knew for himself the rapture of Crossing.

It was as glorious as the First Crossing of his ancestors, for he remembered it well, although it was generations past. The moment had been bequeathed to every child of Cizren by the women of the First Emergence.

When his Grandams had unfolded to Outside for the first time, they were awestruck by the primordial furnace of an eternal universe none of their kind had ever seen, not even in dreams. Normal was the resplendent sapphire suns in the galaxy's heart. Here was long, naked distances between stars, and the galactic darkness of night. Their telepathic minds burned the images into every Cizrenhi left behind. It was a trauma so deep it had changed them on many levels: spiritual, social, even genetic. Everyone carried the new knowledge, and passed it on, and there was no returning to a more innocent age. Now, because there was Outside, there was Inside, and every Cizrenhi confronted a new question: Is Outside a gate opened or a gate closed? The answer was in the heart. The seekers became star nomads. The satisfied stayed home. Nyjehnn was a seeker.

And he dreamt of his Crossing, and the danger: to fly and forget the goal, to be caught in flight and fall too far. There: the two-toned harmonic that was the binary star system he knew as his destination.

The potential energy point slowed his thought. He stopped and unfolded into this universe, which was nothing more than making a decision, like changing your mind. He was created light now. He beamed toward the second, smaller sun, and its single planet Julle, which wore an artificial ring, like a woman engaged to a changeling god. Nyjehnn would've saved her from such folly, but he'd come too late.

Yet, she forgave him. She received him eagerly: Planetfall. The colors! Cobalt, tourmaline, topaz, and alizarin, and jade green, and a million hues more; she wove the global tapestry beneath him. He felt the joyful expectancy to experience sensate flesh again; feet with which to dance; a mouth with which to sing. He dove toward fulfillment in a northern hemisphere ocean, and the delicious shock of rich, organic matter. He fell and her tears welcomed him, and he rested in her tide.

Then came the remembering, the gathering, the mindful task of translating personal vibration to solid flesh. He found the proteins and acids, the minerals and salts, the trace elements necessary for the transformation. He began by exchanging psychic pattern for material tool, slowing and anchoring molecular light, lengthening and dividing living sound. He translated energy to matter at the subchromosomic level, recreating the matrix that was himself before the void.

And he struggled now, to keep himself from returning to the void. It was too soon; his work remained unfinished. He grasped for the energy to stay as a drowning man grasps for any proffered chance to live. He existed at the fulcrum of energy. He was unaware of self, of dark or of light.

All day the air held its breath, and in the hush, waiting was endless and talk an intruder. Brace helped harvest the garden and watched the Cizrenhi go silently about their work, exchanging places at Nyjehnn's bedside.

The vigil had begun after dawn. They stayed with him two hours each and came out looking completely spent. After lunch Brace sought out the Nordawv and found him methodically sweeping the courtyard, and rumbling strangely to himself.

"What's going on?"

The old creature leaned on his brooms. "I am sweeping."

"I mean, with Nyjehnn and his people."

"They are healing him. Don't be concerned. He should be up by this evening."

Marce proved right. At dinner, Nyjehnn came in and sat at the head of the table, nothing of the invalid about him, looking morning fresh in blue watersilk and tans. Cintha sat beside him.

Brace raised his teacup. "Welcome back."

Nyjehnn smiled. "Sorry about that." Khast set a plate of cut fruit and chilled soygurt in front of him.

Everyone else helped themselves to whole-grain and vegetable casserole, hot crusty bread and soft soy cheese. After a bit, Nyjehnn spoke to Brace.

"I want to apologize for what I said last night." He held up his cup as Willa came around, pouring the tea.

Brace swallowed his bread. "What was that?"

"I said that you'd been fighting long enough to realize it was futile to fight. It wasn't my place to say anything."

"You already apologized for that, right after you said it."

"I did?"

"Yes, besides, I've done a lot of thinking today. There's no reason to feel bad about speaking the truth. I guess I've known for a long time how hopeless our chances are, especially now. I just didn't want to see it."

"And you want to go back?"

Brace rubbed his palms together. "I havc to, somehow. I've a ship waiting for me and a duty. I saw something in the Tides before I was captured. I'll be a traitor if I don't get back and report as soon as possible."

Nyjehnn gave Marce a long resigned look.

The Nordawv urged him with a heavy nod.

Nyjehnn finished his last spoonful of fruit. "I know of some people who might supply us a ship."

"Who? Where? Here?"

"Yes, on Julle." He paused. "They're Shaulls."

Brace paled.

"But they're no friend to the City."

Marce spoke. "They've an uneasy truce. In exchange for immunity from slavers and protection from other hostile surface tribes, they work the farms and oil fields in the east. Thus they preserve a measure of freedom for themselves by supplying raw necessities to the City. You understand the politics of placation?"

"Yes," said Brace. "So how can you think they'll help us?"

Nyjehnn leaned forward. "The Refugees have a small secret fleet. I saw it once when I was on patrol. One might assume then, that they have an Underground, that they're already prepared for subversion."

Brace shrugged. "One might also assume that they would do anything to protect that secrecy—from turning us over for a reward to killing us outright."

Cintha's eyes widened and Nyjehnn patted her hand.

"Yes, there's that risk," he said to Brace.

"With your transport trick, why couldn't we slip in and steal one?"

"But that's theft," objected Nyjehnn.

Brace made a wry laugh. "How do you think they probably got that fleet in the first place?"

Nyjehnn considered while he watched Marce drink his tea. Brace got the feeling there was an unheard conversation passing between them.

Aloud, Nyjehnn said. "Can you fly a Shaull craft?"

"Of course. I also speak perfect Sulish."

"We all do."

Brace was taken back. "Then why did you teach me Dhoran?"

"There's more to language than words. Also, we don't use Sulish here anymore. Well, we should leave right away. It's quite a distance, and I'll have to go slow with you along."

Willa interrupted. "Nyjehnn, you should wait a few hours to catch the dawn on your way out."

"Good idea."

Brace scratched his bare palm. "Do you have any weapons?"

Nyjehnn was shocked. "No."

"Oh great! I'm not sneaking into an enemy camp without a weapon. I don't care if it's a table knife." He eyed the one on the cheese plate. "I've got to have something."

"Why?"

"You're serious," observed Brace. "You honestly don't know?"

Nyjehnn glanced at Marce, who was drowsing. He signaled Willa. Released from their dinner manners, Khast took the dishes into the kitchen. LeAnn lit the sunballs. Willa bundled Marce off to bed. Cintha remained beside Nyjehnn. He returned to Brace's question reluctantly.

"I know why you think you need a weapon. But you don't. It's your fear that wants it."

Brace smirked. "Look who's talking. What's wrong with wanting to protect yourself from an enemy?"

"For the Cizrenhi, there's no such person as an enemy."

"You trying to tell me you don't call those traders who killed your father and friends, enemies?"

Nyjehnn shot a look of betrayal at Cintha."When did you tell him?"

"Last night."

Nyjehnn sighed, then leaned on the table. "Let me explain something about self-protection. Violence doesn't work. It's one fire that can't be fought with fire. You only get more flame. Our method of subduing an attacker is called Sant'kye. It's a body discipline and a defensive form of psychic surrender."

"What are you talking about—surrender?"

"Sant'kye's an old word. It means 'quiet hand.' It's best if I show you." He stood and moved into the living room, pulling out the thong that tied back his hair. He put it in his sleeve pocket and took off his boots. "Stand here," he directed Brace. "I'll be careful of your arm."

Brace stood in front of Nyjehnn and flexed his knees.

Nyjehnn breathed deep, sanding his fingertips with his thumbs, raising his level of power a fraction. He lifted his arms over his head in an arc like a bird stretching his wings. "It's a law of nature," he said, "that the stronger, to survive, surrenders to the weaker. Say you have a sword. Strike at me."

Brace swung at Nyjehnn backhanded. Nyjehnn bent before the blow, a movement of total grace. He touched Brace on the ankle. It lost strength, and Brace sat on the mat.

"The tree that resists the wind," he helped Brace to stand, "is uprooted and dies. The truth is in the staying."

There was nothing wrong as Brace tested his ankle.

"Momentary nerve block," explained Nyjehnn. "Lunge at me."

Brace made to run him through. Nyjehnn twisted inside his reach, and they stood as dance partners. He pinched Brace's wrist and it lost its power to grip. He opened his long-fingered hand.

"Take the rock. It's harder than water, yet water wears it away. But then, you see, the channel it cuts becomes the path the water must accept. We use a method of influence, the power of choice. What are you feeling right now?"

"I feel like laughing."

"Yes, I choose to make this a game." He stepped back.

The giddy feeling of play faded, and Brace stood with a puzzled knot between his brows.

Nyjehnn continued."Let me ask you a question. When you saw me in the ship, why didn't you attack? It was dark. I was standing over you, reaching for you. Wouldn't it have been a normal thing for you to do?"

"Yes, I guess. It all happened so fast." He rubbed the back of his neck, thinking out the confusion of that night. "Yes, when I looked up, I was calculating if I could take you with one arm. I knew my left was broken. But then you grabbed me and I felt . . . different. I knew somehow, you were there to help, that you weren't . . . my . . . enemy." Brace said the last three words slowly, realizing how the influence and surrender had felt that night: gentle as a caring mother, selfless as a lover. In remembering, he compared that with the emotion tonight, a carefully controlled aura that had the power to influence by touch. This was the power that Nyjehnn possessed. "How do you do it?"

Nyjehnn shrugged. "I was taught an attitude of choosing to be defenseless. The opponent fights only himself. I'll be your weapon. You won't need another."

Brace still had doubts. "But you couldn't even protect yourself against those traders."

"Who said I didn't. They didn't kill me."

"How did you stop them?"

Nyjehnn rubbed his face. "I can't talk about that, I really can't." He walked to the back windows and stared outside. It was dark and his reflection stared back.

Brace looked at Cintha. "I'm sorry."

Cintha's eyes were tuned to her brother. "I'll go out with you, tonight."

"You will not." His denial was swift.

"I must, Nyjehnn."

"Why?" asked Brace.

She stared through him. "Because I've seen myself there."

Brace felt a glacier crawl down his neck. Nyjehnn made no further objections. Cintha folded her napkin with nervous fingers and stood. "We have a few hours to relax. I need music."

She disappeared halfway across the room. Nyjehnn shook off his mood and stretched. He sat on one of the large floor pillows in the corner of the living room and indicated the pillow on his right. "Make yourself comfortable. Do you like music?"

Brace came across the room. "Very much."

"Cintha's a master of the singing drum. I wish she played more often. I wouldn't want her to lose the gift. She's promised to found a school when we return home." LeAnn and Khast came in from the kitchen and sat across from them.

Brace had to ask. "You aren't going to let Cintha come with us, are you?"

"If I tell her no, she'll follow me anyway. I've never been able to dissuade her from anything she's wanted to do."

Cintha appeared in the center of the room. She had changed her work wist and apron for a silken, teal-blue kimono with a darker sash. Her fine hair was loose. In one hand she held a blackwood frame and drumwand, in the other, a wide, stringed drum. She knelt and settled the instrument in its tilted frame.

After a moment of total stillness, she drummed a slow, hollow beat that stretched the air of the room across a vast desert plain. She plucked a sparse melody in climbing notes of a minor key. The clear tones quivered on the counterpoints—a sound unique to the Cizrenhi singing drum.

The song held Brace entranced in a journey under blue-fire skies, through sparkling mountains and bright mists heady with the scent of the sea. The drumbeat became a thrumming as Cintha wove rhythm and melody with skilled ease, sliding the notes from tension to peace, resonating them hypnotically against the drumhead. Chosen harmonies sank through their sharps to their naturals below and soared up again, lifting the world with them.

The spell cleared and Brace became aware that the four Cizrenhi were chanting. Alternate lines echoed across the music between the women and men. He didn't understand the words, didn't even try, but he recognized the path they uncovered in his mind; it was the way in—to his center, to home. It filled him with the first peace he'd known since leaving his long childhood afternoons of wandering through golden fields.

The song ended as it had begun, on a slow, fading beat. In the sudden stillness, Brace felt sad and more than a little homesick. But he wished her to play it again.

Suddenly a quick and familiar pain burst in him. He slapped his hand to the back of his neck.

"No!" He tried to stand but toppled over.

Nyjehnn stood above him.

Just as quickly, the seizure stopped. It left Brace shaky. He let out a sobbing breath, "Damn."

Nyjehnn helped him to sit upright. "What is it?"

"They're coming."

"Who?"

"The Shaull. They know where I am. It's the finder. I've got to leave now." He started to rise but Nyjehnn held him down.

"What's a finder?"

"A leash. They put it here." He touched his neck behind his right ear. "If they find me here, they'll destroy you, this whole place."

Cintha's drumwand jarred against the strings. Khast and LeAnn both looked stricken and left the room abruptly. Nyjehnn silently summoned Willa. "Why didn't you warn me about this?"

Brace shot him a puzzled look."I thought you knew. You said you were all telepaths."

"I didn't know."

"I was looking for the control pen. The ship blew up, you said, so I thought I was free."

"Telepathy doesn't work unless there's a willingness to communicate."

"I wasn't hiding it," defended Brace.

"I know." Willa rushed in with her box. Nyjehnn motioned her over. "What can you tell me about it?"

"The Shaull use them to control their slaves and

prisoners. It punishes with pain. It can paralyze and it can kill."

Nyjehnn spoke to Willa. "Some kind of neural transponder chip . . . here." He touched Brace behind the ear. "See if you can remove it."

Willa knelt down and opened the lid of her box.

Brace shied back impatiently. "It's too late now. They have a reading. I don't know its range. They could be here at any moment." He looked at Cintha. "I don't want you involved in this, Nyjehnn . . . any of you."

"We already are," said Willa. "Let me see that chip."

Nyjehnn held her back. "No, he's right. They'll track him here. We'll have to lead them away first, then lose them. You must come with us."

Brace leaned forward. "You risk too much. It's better I leave alone."

Nyjehnn stated the obvious. "Is there anyplace you could go where they would not find you?"

"No," admitted Brace.

"Then why refuse my help? This is why I'm here. It's why you're here." He turned to Willa. "Are you ready?"

"Just let me get some kiths." Willa snapped closed the lid.

Nyjehnn put on his boots.

PETAL THE EIGHTEENTH

They arrowed across the eastern alpine range and spotted the ugly black smear scarred along its forested flank. Mazzad descended over the crash site. The early morning was overcast.

"Well, so much for soft landings," she remarked. She hadn't had any real hope; the Oncom channels were dead quiet. She banked lower and set down inside the burn. The other Wing followed her pattern and landed beside them. The ash looked damp and cold, the wreckage twisted and ripped apart, unrecognizable.

"It looks bad," said Dalt. He was properly uniformed and sitting behind the lance officer in the weapons pit.

Mazzad unstrapped from the pilot's pit. "I want proof. Use a sieve if you have to."

Dalt supervised the search. Three hours later they'd found the remnants of one body. He gave Mazzad the bad news. She was pacing the bridge and looked both nervous and exhausted.

"You're certain it's Carnet?"

"Yes." The dress blues made his eyes intense.

She swore and took a control pen from her uniform pocket. She removed the inner cartridge and snapped it into a console card, then inserted it into the navigation's homing unit and activated it. There was no response. She sat at the helm.

"Damn. He couldn't have gotten out of range on foot. He's not dead." She tapped the indicators. "So where is he?" She rubbed her eyes, desparingly.

"How long've you been wearing the stimulant?"

Mazzad sighed and looked at her wrist clip. "About twenty-four hours."

"You need to rest," observed Dalt.

"I need my prisoner." She stared at the blank tracer. "We'll just have to search for him."

"Let the pilot fly. I can call you when we find something. The sooner you get off that, the better."

"I know. All right." She stood and peeled off the patch, pressing the intercom at the same time. "Launch alert, all stations." She turned to Dalt. "I'll be in my cabin."

The ship pressurized as the outer hatch was secured. The two-man crew penetrated the sudden quiet of the bridge, strapping in and beginning their preflight check. Dalt gave them the search orders and left to check on Seyone.

He stepped into her small cabin behind the galley. She was awake and sitting up, wrapped to the chin in her white blankets and staring at the night-light beside her bunk. She'd been crying and was still sniffing dryly. There was a packet of tissues beside her.

He sat on the bunk. "You warm enough?"

She nodded.

"It's good to cry. I'd be worried if you didn't."

She drew up her knees and hugged them. "It's useless."

"Why do you say that?"

"Because it doesn't change anything." She hid her face between her arms. "I ought to know better." She began to cry anyway. "He was a good man. He didn't want to hurt me, or you."

"He was the cadet who followed you."

"Yes." She reached for a tissue, and he gave her one. "I mean, no. Oh, I'm thinking so much, I can't think. He said he was a keftain. But he was wearing a cadet uniform, wasn't he?" She sighed, forcefully. "What does it matter? He's dead." She burst out in tears again.

Dalt began to wonder if there was more behind this trauma than last night's events. "Did you know him, Seyone?"

She calmed and shook her head. "No. He just seemed . . . nice. He said you were smart."

"He knew me?"

"He was listening to you and Mazzad on the bridge. You said something about too few Hendars, and he said, 'Dalt's smart.' "

Dalt sat thinking a long moment. Mazzad had come on board, talking about the delay that evasion had cost her in getting back from the Winter Palace, about her uncle's assassination and the attempt on her life, and her suspicions about the family. The last part hadn't rung true to him. It wasn't logical. The Hendar Dynasty was ruthless in its politics, but never in its family relations. Why would they risk destroying their own power? Dalt figured it had to be someone or something outside, wanting to see the Dynasty fall, wanting to take its place, maybe.

He put a soothing hand on Seyone's head. She looked wrung out. "One more question. Who hired him? Did he say?"

"I don't think it was like that. I can't stop hearing him." She pressed her fists to her head. "He asked me if I wanted freedom. He said he was a keftain in the World Refugee Corps." She opened her hand. "He gave me his rank ring. I don't know why. You take it." She put it in his palm.

Dalt looked at the gold and felt the chill of recognition. Of course, "keftain" was an old term of rank still used by the O'Nel, but no longer valid in the Shaull military. But "Refugee" was a term sometimes used by the surface miners and refinery workers. What did the two have in common? The possibilities of unknown powers, alliances, and conspiracies frightened him. If only Mazzad hadn't been so quick to use the cage. She was myopic in her methods of extracting information. Pain wasn't always the best tool. His attempts to convince her of that had met with threats to break his rank.

He tousled Seyone's hair and pulled a sedative from his belt pack. "You try to get some more rest." He put the patch on her wrist, replacing the old one.

She sighed and lay down. Dalt arranged her covers and strapped her in. She was already asleep. He closed her hatch as he left. He didn't want the galley noise to wake her. It was time to heat some lunch for the crew and himself.

Dalt spent the long hours of search on the bridge, watching the land speed under them, watching the tracer scope, questioning things he thought he knew, like the lives of the Shaull who still lived on the surface. He had been on medical outreach visits a number of times. A farm had looked like a farm, a mine like a mine. Were their junkyards clever shams? He wished he knew more.

The tracer beeped, startling him. He directed the pilot to circle and buzzed Mazzad's cabin. She was slow to answer.

Dalt said, "The reading's faint but steady. I think we've found him."

"I'll be right there."

A few minutes later, she stalked onto the bridge like a jagar hungry for her prey. She studied the scope over Dalt's shoulder. After finding Carnet's cinders and hours of delay, she was more than ready for the kill.

"Turn up the frequency, Dalt."

He increased the power to the homing unit.

Mazzad watched the scope focus. "Got him!" She fisted her palm. The O'Nel would be hers at last. She pulled the search pilot out of the pit and clambered in. The coordinates were on the screen. She keyed them into the Oncom and grabbed the controls. The ship swung in response, and the whine of the engines filled the cabin. Mazzad pointed the Wing west and flew confidently over the night-scaped continent. She welcomed the sensual sating that flooded her whenever she took the helm. She gave the engines more thrust and smiled.

"Hard deck, everybody," she warned, and buckled her own straps. She pulled the Sprint over a tight wingtip roll, did an outside loop, and spun her upright. Flying quenched her lust for power. Nothing else came as close. She leaned back, satisfied and relaxed, and hummed along with the engines.

Dalt sat in the navigator's pit, watching the scope. The light winked out. "Huh? Mazzad, it just disappeared."

"It what?" Mazzad whirled around.

"It's off the scope."

"That's impossible. Check your station." She keyed in a monitor. "Widen the band."

He did. "Nothing. I can't understand it. Wait, there it is." Dalt puzzled over the screen. "This is crazy. He's twenty mects north, just like that."

Mazzad thumped her scope. "Bring the signal up by two. I want it certain." She punched in Oncom and wondered where he'd gotten a ship. The Sprint swung around under her grip.

"What?" Dalt fumed. "It's gone again."

"Cut it. Get a relay from Orbitspy." Mazzad slapped on the big screen and got the western half of the continent in weak infrared. She pointed. "There he is. Thirty mects east." She watched as the blip winked out, then reappeared another ten mects northeast in a matter of seconds.

"What kind of ship is that?" asked Dalt.

Mazzad opened the throttle. "Just don't lose him. I'm not going back empty-handed."

PETAL THE NINETEENTH

Nyjehnn's breath frosted the moonlight spilling through the broken windows of the vacant warehouse shell. Cintha and Willa stood on the dusty concrete behind him. He knelt over Brace, who lay curled on the littered floor, and pulled back the hood of his kith. Brace was only semiconscious, every muscle of his body a screaming knot in the vise of the Shaull's finder.

Willa knelt and urged. "It's got to come out now."

"Yes, quickly." He pried Brace's hands away.

Willa bent and stroked his neck just below the right mastoid process, probing for the chip. A small lump appeared and glowed green light through the skin. Brace sobbed and slumped unconscious. Nyjehnn held him. Willa chose a thin blade and cloth square from her box. She deftly removed the transparent chip, catching the blossom of blood with the self-stick patch. The chip was dark now. She dried it with another cloth.

"What is this?" She handed it to Nyjehnn.

"Brace called it a leash." He turned it over, examining it. "It doesn't call outside the body. Good."

"Throw it away." Willa closed her box.

"I will, but not now. We'd better go. Our trail ends here." He put the chip in his kith pocket and shook Brace gently. Willa passed her hand over Brace's forehead and he woke groggily.

Nyjehnn helped him to stand. "It's all right now."

Brace touched the bandage. "The finder?"

"Willa freed you of it. But here was its last signal. We've got to jump."

As Nyjehnn led them out of the ruins, an owl soared over their heads, hunting on silent wings and, just as silently, winging into the night. They climbed to higher ground behind the rusting building. From there Nyjehnn sighted the next destination, a snowy mountain range across thirty miles of deserted industrial valley. They linked hands and disappeared in shimmering moonlight.

A few seconds later, they stood on a bare rock promontory above a narrow pass. An abandoned roadway, fissured by saplings and ice, gleamed silver under the westerly moon. The highway raked across the pass and down through the dark evergreens on the other side. The sky in the east was growing light.

Brace felt like a man trying to read a picture book when someone else is turning the pages too fast. Just as he was able to make sense of the landscape, Nyjehnn would flip the page. It was extremely confusing and taxing on the brain. It worked better if he kept his eyes closed. He opened his eyes, and Nyjehnn pointed to the next fold of hills.

"One more jump to dawn—there."

Brace looked and saw a triangle-shaped mountain with a bare crown above the treeline. Then the dizzy, shifting rush of the jump blurred his vision and he closed his eyes again.

His ears popped and he felt springy grass under his boots. He looked around; they were on the distant summit, smelling the moss and crisp alpine air. The eastern sky was aqua now with a blush of watery gold.

Nyjehnn cupped his hands and steamed them warm. He looked down into the blue, shadowed valley. "Sunrise in a few minutes, then we'll go on. See that wisp of smoke beyond the river?"

"Is that the Refugees?" asked Brace.

"One of their mines. The base is beyond those mesa cliffs." He nodded toward the horizon. "Only one more jump, I promise." He pulled back his hood.

"I think I'm getting used to them."

Nyjehnn turned to Brace and froze in astonishment. "Don't move," he whispered. "A quill bear's behind you. Don't—"

But it was too late. Brace spun around. The animal roared and charged at them.

"Willa!" Nyjehnn warned. He grabbed for Brace but missed. Willa and Cintha disappeared.

"Run!" ordered Nyjehnn. Brace stumbled back. The bear was between them. It swung a massive paw, hit Nyjehnn full in the chest, and flung him high. He landed hard and rolled to a limp stop. The animal roared again and rocked on its hind paws, deciding its prey.

Brace jumped up and waved his arms. "Hoa! Bear!"

The bear lunged toward him. Brace turned and ran. He opened a promising distance, but then tripped on a rock. He scrabbled back until he found the dislodged stone. In one instinctive move, he rose, aimed, and threw the crude weapon. It smashed its target in the left eye. The animal dropped in a skidding nose dive. Brace retrieved the rock as the bear clawed the ground, struggling to rise. He darted in quick and struck at the skull until the beast was dead.

He sagged to his knees, gasping the painfully cold air, shaking, aware of an ache in his healing arm and countless heightened sensations. He remembered Nyjehnn and toiled up the steep hill.

"Nyjehnn?" He bent and pulled him onto his back. A sudden presence made him look up.

Cintha stood over him, holding Willa's hand, staring at him with a familiar horror. Her gaze lowered to his right hand.

Brace looked down to see he still held the rock. It was bloody. "I killed him."

Cintha inhaled sharply.

"The bear." He tossed the rock down the slope and pointed to the dark mound. "See?"

She glanced wordlessly at his directing. The sun cleared the horizon and burnished the quilled fur golden.

"Thank the Lady," breathed Cintha. She and Willa pivoted to the sunrise. Like sleepwalkers captured by vision, they stood entranced by the light. Willa held Cintha's hand. With their free hands, they undid their long silk hair. It lifted on slow, invisible waves, becoming alive, moving as if it were being washed in a tide.

Brace called their names. They were oblivious to him. He filed through all their references to dawn and sunlight—winter, something about winter, and the times he's seen them touch their sunball lights; he'd touched one and nothing had happened. It came to him that they used and were dependent somehow on the sun's energy. They had timed the trip to meet this dawn. He sat on his heel and shook Nyjehnn urgently. He was already waking.

"Nyjehnn, get up. Hurry." He helped him up.

The pain in Nyjehnn's eyes cleared as he recognized the dawn. He untwined his braid and became a statue with bright, cumulus hair.

It made Brace nervous, this defenselessness of theirs. Suppose there was another bear? He unbuttoned his kith and surveyed the treeline below him.

The next moment, the two women lowered their eyes and turned to him. For a moment they looked like people he'd never met; there was a newness about them. Then their hair quieted and he recognized them.

Cintha sighed and smiled at him. "This is what I saw in my dream. I'm sorry for believing you would hurt my brother."

"You mean this . . . ? "He gestured at the bear in surprise.

"Yes. You were defending him, not. . . . Thank you."

"That's okay. I'm relieved it's over."

Nyjehnn came out of Sunning. Willa reached for him. "Are you all right?" She did a quick mental scan.

He pressed a hand to the front of his kith. "Fine. A few sore ribs is all." He looked at Brace. "What happened?"

Brace pointed down slope. "I had to kill him."

"Had to?" Nyjehnn walked down to the dead animal. He knelt and stroked the lifeless quilled paw.

Brace came beside him. "Not enough time for your 'influence' to work?"

There was an edge of impatient anger in his voice.

"Understand this: your influence caused the attack. She was only the water in the rock."

"I know what I saw. The bear attacked you."

Nyjehnn shook his loose hair. "No. She pushed me out of the way." He stood up. "I'm not really blaming you. You both did what you had to do. Don't you see the prison in that?"

Brace folded his arms. "I don't know what you mean. But 'Thank you anyway, Brace, for saving my life, not to mention your own.' " There was a shade of irony in his voice.

Nyjehnn puzzled over his words a moment then relaxed and smiled. "Yes, I owe you that. I am thankful."

"We're even." He dismissed it and looked across the valley, eager to go on.

Nyjehnn agreed. "Let's get this finished." They returned to the women. He took Cintha's hand. "It would be easier for me if you would let Willa take you home."

"Wait." Brace tapped his bandage. "Damn, of course. You know what the Shaull will do?"

"What?"

"They've lost something, right? They'll back-track and check every place they spotted the signal."

Nyjehnn started. "I never thought of that."

"I didn't expect you would. We need to get that ship fast and track them down before they find your Keep."

"And then what?"

"You know very well what I must do. Nyjehnn, you can't fight machines. They don't have feelings."

"I can't allow myself to become an accomplice to war." His hand strayed into his pocket.

"How about a partner to murder? They'll burn your people right off the map."

Nyjehnn opened his palm and looked at the chip.

Brace stared. "You still have it?"

"I couldn't throw it away. There's a ship on the other end."

Brace understood. "That's suicide."

"I don't know. But I can't negotiate for a Refugee ship now. There's no time. I've no other choice." He turned to Willa. "Put this in me."

Cintha was horrified. "No!"

Willa shrank back. "I will not."

"I want it transmitting only, not controlling. Put it here, in my arm." He pushed up his right sleeve.

Brace lunged forward, reaching for the chip. Nyjehnn stepped back and ducked. Brace landed in the moss.

He rolled over. "You're crazy. Don't do this."

Nyjehnn pulled him up and looked hard in his face. "You want to find the enemy so badly? Look in a mirror. You'll see our common enemy—fear. I admit it. But now, I'm finished running. Six years is long enough." He let go of Brace. "Do it, Willa, or I will take a blade and do it myself."

Willa shuddered. "No. I will do it."

"Hurry." He laid the chip on his scarred wrist.

Willa pressed her thumb over it and concentrated for ten beats of his pulse. She had cared for him since his birth; his body was as familiar as her own. It was a simple task to pierce the epidermis, molecule by molecule, to coax the well-known cells aside, layer by layer and smooth them together again. When she lifted her thumb, the chip blinked bright green beneath his unbroken skin.

"Good." He turned to Cintha. "When I've diverted them, take Brace back to the Keep. I'll be in touch. Don't worry."

Cintha hugged him and he was overwhelmed by her flood of wordless longing for his safety.

"Trust," he reminded her.

She nodded and let him go. He whirled and vanished from the morning.

"Trust," snorted Brace. "Only children believe trust can defend them from chance. And chances are excellent the Shaull will capture your brother." He stepped closer to Cintha. "They are like nothing you can imagine. They worship randomness. It allows them to be irresponsible. That's why they're such good killers. Nyjehnn's no match for them."

"They won't kill him. They won't capture him." She groped for and found Willa's hand.

"Do you really believe that?" Brace was losing his patience."If he only wanted to divert them, how did he plan on removing the finder?"

All the light went out of Cintha and she turned to Willa. "We must go for Marce."

"I'll go. But you could trace Nyjehnn yourself by his harmonics."

"How can I without you?"

Willa considered Brace. "He has good eyes." She took a small medkit from her box and handed it to him. "Will you let her use your eyes? Will you help us save Nyjehnn?"

"Yes. We can try."

Cintha panicked. "His eyes, his hands are so strange."

Willa backed out of her reach and she groped blindly. Brace caught her hand. "Don't be afraid."

"I'm not afraid for myself." She kept her eyes averted. "Don't look at me, please."

He glanced at Willa, who smiled encouragingly and then disappeared.

Brace felt an unfamiliar shyness and a gentle presence inside him. It was not Cintha herself, but a feeling that he was the flower and she the fragrance. The mountain slope and the treeline below them became more defined, their rugged colors more intense.

"Northeast," directed Cintha and she turned with him.

Brace was aware of an echo of longing too swift for him to follow. It arrowed out across the valley and the northern hills.

She whispered. "So far, so soon." And she warned him. "His first jump was a long one. Ready?"

"No, but let's do it."

Nyjehnn traveled east and the deeper he penetrated the wide continent, the tighter winter gripped the sky and land. The desolate landscape was frozen in colors of iron and ice. He stood now, undecided on the rim of a narrow canyon watching the river below turning brittle with the advancing cold. Ahead, there was a blizzard blocking his route, a big one. Continuing east would cost him time. He would need to take more care in the sightings and use shorter jumps to conserve energy. He thought about turning south, but that way led to the sea. Maybe a storm would slow his pursuers too. It was a chance.

He jumped across the canyon into the first flurries. Heading into the wind, he turned more northward, keeping to the fringes. Still, the snow was deep and had no surface tension; he stood in knee-deep drifts. The wind flung stinging snow out of the icy whiteness. He drew his hood down and jumped blindly, using memory only. He landed and stumbled to his hands and knees.

The snowpack was less deep and the visibility was better. His small reserve of energy was depleting, but he took heart at the improved conditions and struck out east again. He was on the last open ground before the eastern range, a barrier with barbs piercing three miles into the clouds.

Let them fly through that, thought Nyjehnn. But suddenly a blazing light plunged down on him from overhead and an abrupt numbness seized him and he fell into cold oblivion.

PETAL THE TWENTIETH

Mazzad watched her two crewmen exit and approach her numbed captive lying in the snowdrift. Daytime visibility was bad even with the ship's lights trained on the scene. There was no sign of a vehicle of any kind. She tripped the external speakers.

"Get him in the outer hatch first. Then you can wake him up and search him." She turned to Dalt. "Better make sure he's alert."

"Yes, Mazzad." Dalt left.

Mazzad waited at the helm, tapping out her rising impatience. Her short rest had done little to restore her nerves. Setbacks and frustrations had sapped her sense of control right from the moment she'd come home. What she needed most was a quiet vacation back at the Front.

There were footsteps in the passageway, and Dalt and the other crewmen marched in with the prisoner. He was the wrong man.

She stared. "Who is this?"

"The prisoner we've been chasing all over the continent." Dalt deliberately kept his voice level and calm.

Mazzad shot out of her command chair. "Explain this! We chase my finder, the one I implanted." She held up the card from the homing unit on the console. "And when we catch up with it, we find this? Does it look like an O'Nel to you?" She presented Nyjehnn for Dalt's inspection.

He stepped away from the prisoner, taking no more than a dutiful glance. If the cargo was going to invoke her temper, he wanted some distance. He made an attempt to placate her.

"No, Pack Reeve. But the fact is, your finder led directly to him. There was no ship. There was no one else."

Mazzad humphed and glowered at Nyjehnn. He was a strange being. Tall and thin, his long hair hung in disarray down his shirt. He was almost too bright for her eyes. She squinted as his wrist caught her attention. She grabbed it up for a closer look.

"Yes, the O'Nel's finder. You must've taken it from him. How? Where is he?" She stared at him, watching his eyes, looking for fright, or evasion, or . . . His eyes were strange, too. They seemed . . . She became aware that she was holding an alien's hand. A race she'd never seen before. An odd sensation spread inside her. She looked up again to see his dark glinting eyes on her, eyes the color of space shadows on the far side of asteroids. And he wore a disturbingly intimate smile on his handsome face.

Mazzad dropped his hand abruptly and wiped hers on the front of her uniform to disguise her trepidation.

"Replace the finder where it belongs, Dalt."

Her medic did as he was told. Nyjehnn pressed the bleeding punctures and regarded the implant device with disdain. Dalt swabbed his wrist and neck with a germicide wipe, and stepped out of the way.

Mazzad controlled her frustration with difficulty. "Where is the O'Nel?" But she was glad to be angry again, to feel something familiar.

Dalt ventured, "I wish I knew."

"I wasn't talking to you. Shut up. He knows." She pointed at the quiet prisoner, permitting herself to speak to him. "And you will tell me where my property is or I will burn your brain right out of your skinny skull."

She paced in front of the bridge shield, watching him from the corner of her eyes for . . . what? She didn't know really—some kind of reaction.

Dalt, too, leaning against the navigator's console, was studying thc prisoncr's attitude. He seemed too unconcerned, too uninvolved. That kind of apathy was common in slaves. Was he a decoy? But who would sacrifice someone so perfect? "Mazzad, I don't think he understands our language."

Mazzad swore. "What does that matter? He wears the O'Nel's finder. I think he knows exactly what I want. Show him a map."

Dalt turned to the com station and in a second had a printout. He handed the warm page to Nyjehnn.

Nyjehnn sensed the tension surrounding him. They were wary, on the edge, a step from fear, a step from violence. Afraid of him, an unknown. The knowledge filled him with wonder. Is this how Brace had felt, confronted by the Cizrenhi's fear? He puzzled over the strength of their illusion as he took the map and glanced over the wide continent. He recognized only the locations of his Keep and his route. He questioned Mazzad with a look and pointed to the deck and then to the map. It might be wise to let them think he was ignorant of Sulish.

Mazzad grabbed the map, looked and sighed in exasperation.

"Dalt, mark our present location as a reference." She threw the paper at him and resumed her pacing.

She's a trip wire waiting for one false step, thought Dalt. He circled the spot and gave it back to the prisoner, who stood calmly. Dalt knew that composure was increasingly irritating to the Pack Reeve. She enjoyed a captive's fear, but this one didn't act like a prisoner at all, and that was adding to her present frustration. It made the whole atmosphere of the bridge unbalanced somehow. He felt sorry for the prisoner.

Nyjehnn reexamined the map, relieved at the distance between the Shaull and his Keep. He looked up. Mazzad was watching him with a hungry expectation. There was no way not to provoke her. Might as well be clear. He crumpled the paper and dropped it at her feet.

The nearest crewman reacted with a fast hard jab to Nyjehnn's ribs. But Nyjehnn stepped back just as quickly, twisted inward and grabbed the man's elbow. Before the lance officer knew what had happened, he found himself on the deck. He jumped up, weapon in hand.

"No!" shouted Mazzad. "No more of that. I don't want this one damaged. I want answers this time."

The officer lowered his weapon.

"Now." Mazzad scooped up the map and held it out to Nyjehnn. "I warn you. If I have to ask you again about my O'Nel, it won't be with words."

He remained silent, regarding her calmly.

Mazzad avoided his intense eyes and sighed. "No, is it? All right. Take him to the cage. I'll be right there."

The crewmen ushered Nyjehnn off the bridge.

Mazzad threw the crumpled map and Dalt caught it. "Maybe," he said, "you should wait on the cage—"

She interrupted him. "Maybe you should remember who has the rank on board. I recall, now, why I disliked working with you. You haven't changed. You've still got too many scruples for a good pack officer. Just do your job, medic."

The light in the interrogation lounge was dim ruby on the hatch side, and bright, hot red on the other. It was the wrong spectrum for Nyjehnn, and he shuddered from the rasp of it against his exposed skin.

The lanceman laughed. "Not so calm now, are you?"

Nyjehnn concentrated on his breathing to disassociate his senses from the assaulting light. The officer kicked the base of the platform and the glass front rose silently. He shoved Nyjehnn into the cage when the lower edge cleared his height. Nyjehnn turned and watched it descend again. From this side he could see the glass was honeycombed with tiny liquid marbles. He knew then what they meant to do. They used sound in a perverted form.

He sat down, drawing his legs under him, and closed his eyes. He pulled himself in, gathering what little energy remained after the long chase and capture, freeing it from the emotions for the test ahead, a necessity he'd learned long ago. Emotions were fickle tools. They could please you or destroy you. Detachment was the only way to survive.

The air around him began to hum, rising to a kind of dancing life of its own. He opened his eyes to see the Pack Reeve enter, fresh map in hand.

She stopped in front of him. "Stand up!" She demanded.

He ignored her.

She shrugged. "No matter. I like looking down at you. Any second thoughts?"

She sighed over his silence. "All right. Dalt, take the controls." She made herself comfortable in one of the soft chairs, stretching out and crossing her boots. The toes almost touched the glass of the cage. She laid the map in the chair next to her.

"Give him sone three, just to make a good first impression."

There was a louder hum in the room. Mazzad waited, watching her prisoner for . . . Nothing. "Is that thing working?"

"Yes."

"Sone five, then." This time she was rewarded as Nyjehnn swayed and recovered. She signaled Dalt to cut power and leaned forward. She tapped the glass with her toe.

"The sones go up to twenty, but I've rarely seen ten. They die before that with quite a bit of begging and screaming. This machine has an affinity for certain very sensitive nerves, and death is extremely painful." She tapped the glass again."Would you like to look at the map?"

Nyjehnn opened his dark eyes slowly. They bored through her, skewering her to the chair like a moth to a mounting board.

She tore her eyes away from him, hunkered back in the chair, and hissed in an angry breath: "Sone seven!"

The humming climbed to a keening pitch, piercing Nyjehnn with pain. The cage worked in tandem with the finder, making a double assault. He closed his eyes, eager for the darkness of his own reality. He concentrated on his breath, placing his awareness within it. He was the breath. He came in and went out. He did not live in the body. The body was pain. He brought his hands together in his lap, fingertips touching, connecting, completing a second energy flow—a countercurrent, but weaker. How long he could continue it, he didn't know.

PETAL THE TWENTY-FIRST

Brace found it easier this time, with Cintha turning the landscape pages. Slower, because she cast ahead on some inner communion level that excluded him even while she searched the world through his eyes. But her urgent intimacy also included him. She held him in a psychic embrace of purified passion. He felt her feelings as if they were his own. He was desperate for the safety of his beloved brother, yet he knew he had no brother. He was frightened that when he found him, it might be too late.

They stood against an icy wind, facing an endless stretch of foothills mounded with snow. The blizzard was losing its force, snowing quietly now. Darkness was descending early.

"Into that?" asked Brace.

"Yes." She squeezed his hand and he felt the familiar tension of prejump, then the scene swirled, changed, and steadied, and they were on a wind-bare cliff overlooking two gleaming Sprints on the soft plain below.

Brace pulled Cintha behind a frozen ragbush. She was shivering, but happy.

"I found him. Thank you." She hugged him.

"I wish it weren't so cold for you."

"Don't worry about me. Let's get Nyjehnn."

"Stay here out of the wind." Brace crept to the edge of the cliff and squinted through the sifting snow, studying the Shaull landing site.

"They'll have Nyjehnn in the Pack Reeve's ship," he called to Cintha. "It's the one on the left.

Cintha was already concentrating in that direction, trying mentally to pluck her brother up to the safety of their ridge. She leaned back despondently.

"He won't let me in, or can't. I don't know. I get warning and rejection. He's exhausted."

Brace was thinking about Shaull interrogation games."Maybe when he's had a chance to recover."

"Recover?" Cintha turned on him. "Not within the ship, cut off from the sun."

"That's right, I forgot."

She came and gripped his hand. "How will we get him out?"

Brace stared out over the site, aware that Cintha was watching him. It made him wonder if she could see into him, now, deeper than his skin; if she saw the fear he felt for Nyjehnn, for all of them. He stroked her hand.

"It isn't going to be simple. You should be prepared for failure." He thought about his capture. "I know these . . . people. And I've come to know

Nyjehnn. Mazzad, the commander, will ask him where I am, and he won't tell her. Forgive me for saying this aloud, but she will torture him, and still he won't speak."

Cintha tried to pull away. "No!"

Brace held her down. "Listen. If he lives . . . Listen to me! If he lives she will sell him in the City to the highest bidder as a body slave. A Shaull knows only rank or profit. Mazzad will take what she can get."

"Dearest Wey! No!" She sprang away and stumbled down a side gully that led to the plain. Brace caught up and pulled her down into the snow, among the ice-cracked boulders. She was crying.

"Let me go! I love him. I'll trade my life for his."

Brace shook her. "No! Stop it!"

She calmed down.

"I love him, too. I'd give myself if I thought it would do any good. But it won't. They're not the kind to honor a trade. Understand? It's me they want, but they won't trade."

The cliffs around them were reflected in her sightless eyes. "No. I don't understand that." She wrenched away and he let go of her. "Then I came to die with him, or be a slave, too." She hugged herself and began to shiver.

Brace's heart fluttered with fear. "No. You don't know what you're saying." Visions crowded his mind, the offhand way of Shaull cruelty. What a sport they could make of two people as beautiful as Cintha and her brother, not to mention the profit.

"You won't be their slave, I promise you that, and neither will Nyjehnn. As long as those ships sit on the ground, we have a chance to save him."

He filled his lungs, weighing on each side the risk and the odds, like breathing in and breathing out. But the balance was hopelessly uneven, and it made him angry.

"Come on." He helped her to stand. She clung to him and he held her gladly. The fear was gone. It had slipped from his heart like an eclipse dropping away from his courage. For the first time since his capture, he felt strong and sure, finally in possession of his destiny.

Cintha stepped back. This close, her eyes had changed again. She lifted her head with determined bravery and looked deep in his eyes.

"When I think of how long I dreaded your coming . . ." She smiled through her tears. "And now I'm thankful you're here."

He didn't know what to say, so he kissed her, gently on the lips. They were soft and warm as a flower petal under the summer sun. He felt a sideslip of vertigo and new thoughts confused him. They were her thoughts: permission and gladness and shy wonder that two so different could be so same. He felt the yes echo between them, and straightened before he lost his balance completely. Her touch was still on his lips, and her gaze was open. When had she taken his hand? What does she see? Everything. He knew it as certainly as he knew they had shared consciousness, had learned each other without speaking a single word. She knew now how much she meant to him. And he knew the transformation of himself in her—the metamorphosis he was undergoing in her emotions; from a man denied, to a man recognized, and swiftly becoming loved.

"Come." She pulled him back toward the cliff, looking back once with a glance of joy.

They climbed together to a lower vantage point on the crumbled cliff face. Brace leaned across a boulder on his stomach and squinted in the fading light at the two Sprints. Underneath one lay a mounded tarp.

Cintha shivered and asked, "What are we waiting for?"

"For dark. They haven't posted guards or sentry beams. Either they're sure of their isolation or they're surveilling from the ships. Night will give us a better chance." Half to himself, he continued. "If only I had a weapon, anything that—" He stumbled over the idea with a growing excitement. "Cintha, your globe lights, sunballs. They're energy, right? Can you make the light without the glass?"

"Of a sort, yes."

Brace grinned. "Maybe we have more than a chance."

PETAL THE TWENTY-SECOND

Mazzad sat drumming out her frustration on the arm of her chair. Who was this being who could sit under a seven and deny her the satisfaction that seven always gave? An O'Nel would be near death by now, begging for an end to the pain.

"Nine," she snapped. Nothing . . . not even a tremble. She leaned forward again. "You will break. You must," she hissed. "Eleven."

Tears slipped down Nyjehnn's cheeks and sweat trailed from his hairline to clenched jaw, the only outward signs of the struggle within.

"Twelve!" Mazzad's voice was becoming shrill.

Dalt interrupted timidly. "Reeve? As medic officer, it's my duty to remind the Pack Reeve that too long at these sones could result in damage to his hearing."

"Shut up! Fourteen!"

Dalt hesitated.

"Fourteen, damn you!"

Dalt complied and Nyjehnn cried out, hands to head. He slumped forward and sideways, unconscious against the glass.

Mazzad pounded the arm of her chair. "Turn it off." She stood and viciously kicked the base. It opened too slowly for her anger and she paced the cabin. "Don't just stand there. Drag him out. Wake him up."

Dalt stepped in and pulled Nyjehnn onto the deck. He took a miniature cylinder from his belt and sprayed its contents in Nyjehnn's face.

He woke, coughing. Dalt helped him to his feet.

Mazzad snatched the map up and thrust it out. "The O'Nel! Show me where he is or we start again."

Nyjehnn braced himself, staring at the deck until the walls quit their spinning. Outwardly he looked calm, but inside he struggled to keep everything of the senses away, to stay empty, clutching this nothingness to his breast like a cocoon.

"Wake up!" Mazzad slapped him. "I will break you, or I will kill you. Take your choice." When she got no response, she signaled to Dalt.

"Wait." Nyjehnn's voice was breathless, but it shocked them to stillness. "You have no power that can force me to betray the O'Nel. If I must, Mazzad, I will choose death."

Mazzad stared, open-mouthed, astonished for the moment by his perfect Sulish and the use of her personal name. Then her rage returned as his challenge became clear.

"How dare you!" She clenched her fist and struck him in the mouth, her multiple rank rings cutting deep.

Nyjehnn crashed to his knees beside Dalt, who held him.

Mazzad grabbed a handful of silver hair and yanked his head back. "You have no choices, O'Nel-lover! I do with you as I please!" She released his limp head. He was out. "Take him to a cell. We'll continue later." She stamped out of the lounge.

In her cabin, she tried to relax. Her mind whirled. No prisoner had ever dared speak to her as this one had. She burned with indignation. How dare he threaten her. She sat up suddenly. How does one threaten with their own death? What kind of weapon was that? She almost snickered, then shook her head. An effective one, she admitted. There was truth in his words. It was strange and irrational, but she knew there was a power in him that she didn't understand. She had felt it when they'd touched. If she pushed the interrogation, he would carry out his threat, somehow.

Why did she care? She, Mazzad, who had killed more enemy than she could tally. Killing was nothing to her. What was it about him? She pressed her hands to her hot face, remembering her rings. She looked at his blood. She pulled them off and washed in the small basin by her bunk. The intercom was there. She dried her hands and buzzed the medbay.

Dalt answered. "Yes, Mazzad."

"Repair the prisoner's face. If I can't break him, I'll sell him. And I don't need a scar subtracting from my profit. We'll write the O'Nel off; he's not going anywhere down here.

"And . . . put a silencer on him. Until he talks to me, he won't talk at all. Understood?"

"Yes."

Mazzad snapped off and sat heavily on her bunk.

There was a timid knock at her cabin door. Her slave inquired from outside.

"Is there anything you desire?"

Mazzad scrubbed her face. Yes, she desired to hurt the prisoner very badly, to make him beg to answer every question she put to him.

"No, Seyone. Go away. I wish to rest."

PETAL THE TWENTY-THIRD

Seyone padded down the corridor. She had been awakened from a sound sleep by the intercom and fearing Mazzad had summoned her, she came in her night robe, which was blue. She was barefoot quiet, but the bell on her right ankle jingled with every step. She came abreast of the medbay and saw Officer Dalt inside, unpacking instruments. She stepped in.

"Hi."

Dalt looked up. "Feeling better?"

"Yes. Thank you for . . ." She was unused to anyone giving her care; she didn't know how to thank him.

"Sure. Just doing my job." He sounded cynical. He stopped what he was doing and leaned on the counter, head down. His voice softened. "I'm sorry, Seyone. I shouldn't take it out on you."

"What's wrong?" She came beside him.

"Mazzad's wrong. I'll be glad when my promotion's cleared. Then the next time she wants a favor, I can say no."

"No, to a Hendar?" The idea was unthinkable to her.

He shrugged. "There's no getting past that, is there?" He sounded hopeless.

"Why don't I bring you a cup of something hot?"

"Thanks, but I'd better get to work."

"I'll bring you something anyway." She left the medbay and continued down the ramp to the lower level. She passed the cell. It wasn't empty anymore. There was someone lying on the floor, someone almost familiar. The recognition hit her suddenly and her knees lost their strength. She grasped the bars as she slid down.

"No. It can't be." She reached toward his slack hand, shyly, feeling for his pulse. Reassured, she pulled a tissue from her pocket and cleaned the blood from his face. I know only one man with hair the color of clouds, she thought. No. I'm dreaming. It's impossible. Yet . . . you feel so real.

She caressed his silk hair and the past rushed into a heart she had shut against it. Her throat ached as the memories of him moved in her mind again. Six years since she'd last seen him. It felt like another lifetime. But to see him here—it broke her heart. He belonged in her dreams of freedom.

She remembered the first breathless moment she saw him at the Chant. All month Cintha had looked for his coming and she'd helped her sew his wardrobe, listening to her stories of him. Maybe she'd fallen in love right then. When she finally saw him, standing under the forest eaves yet surrounded in light, she was certain. And just as certain of its impossibility.

"I tried so hard to forget you," she whispered.

Nyjehnn stirred and opened his eyes. He stared as his vision cleared. "Seyone?"

She leaned away, uncertain of his reaction. "Yes." She held out her tissue. "You're hurt. You shouldn't try to talk."

He sat up and took her hand. "It *is* you." But belief was new and fragile. He was silenced by the years of their separation and the need now to fill himself with the reality of her presence. It felt like a healing, and he smiled despite his hurt.

"I thought I'd never see you again."

"You don't hate me?"

"Hate you?" He was mystified."No. Why?"

Seyone found she couldn't answer. She couldn't make herself speak of the night she thought him dead.

Nyjehnn squeezed her hand. "I never blamed you for that. It wasn't your fault."

"I left them." Her voice was hesitant and soft. "When they came back . . . that night, I asked my father . . ." Tears welled in her eyes.

"Don't."

She touched his hair. "It's grown back. He had your braid. He told me you were dead. That all were dead. Is Cintha . . .?"

"She's fine. LeAnn, Willa, Khast, and Marce." He named the survivors for her.

"Only . . . ?" She looked down at his long, slim hands wrapped in hers. "I cursed the people of my birth. I walked away in the morning. I couldn't live with them after that."

"Where did you go?"

Seyone thought of all the years of loneliness and humiliating slavery. She didn't want to hurt him with the truth. She made it sound adventurous. "I followed the sun into the desert lands, living on my own for a time. Then I joined another caravan, people I didn't know, who didn't know me. I danced, but not well. I guess my heart wasn't in it. They sold me to a slaver. I was taken to the Ringcity and Mazzad bought me. Now I serve her, but I don't mind. I wanted to forget the past and who I was and what I'd come from—all the hate."

"Did you?"

She shook her head and her short black hair swung.

"No, but somewhere in the years of my thoughts, the hate turned to understanding and I felt compassion for them. I think they weren't so much evil as frightened, and frightened people can do terrible things." She gave him a gentle look.

Nyjehnn stiffened. "You're excusing them?"

"No." She shrugged. "Forgiving them."

For a moment he looked utterly lost from her, as if she had disappeared suddenly, and he was alone in the world. Then he closed and opened his dark eyes.

"I envy you. I wish I could forgive them. I've tried." His voice dropped to a whisper. "The Lady knows, I've tried."

His plea made her ache inside. He started to pull his hand from hers. She saw then, the scars on his wrist. "What did they do to you, Nyjehnn?"

He spoke to the deck, and his hair obscured his face.

"They let me survive and it wasn't right. I shouldn't have. Father, little Lita . . . they should be alive, not me."

"Don't say that. I'm so glad you live. I only wish . . ." She looked around the cell. "You shouldn't be here. Why are you?"

He stared up at the overhead light a moment. "Their lights are dead. Did you know that? There's no healing in them. It's as if they want only to see other things, but not themselves."

"Yes, that's true."

"I came for a friend. It would've been fatal for him to face them, so I came in his place."

She wanted to understand, but she couldn't grasp what he was talking about. He seemed absorbed in thought.

"It's not fatal for you?"

"No. I don't think it will come to that."

"You don't know them. Go away, Nyjehnn, while you can."

He shook his head. "I have a finder. It would be a waste of energy to run away."

She pressed herself against the cell and pulled him close. He responded gently and she held him, her forehead to his, through the bars. The bright closeness of him overwhelmed her. Was it her trembling or his?

"It's all right." She thought, now, at this moment, yes, everything is right. But her mind raced, trying to think of ways to free him.

Then she heard someone coming down the ramp and the slave in her jumped with fright. She kissed his wrist quickly and sprang away, her bell ringing faintly down the corridor.

Dalt came and opened Nyjehnn's cell by entering a sequence of numbers into the lock.

"I'm the medical officer," he said.

Nyjehnn stood up. "Yes, I know. You're Dalt."

The medic hesitated a moment. "Yes. If you'll come with me, I'll fix that cut." They went up to the medbay.

"Lie on the table, please." Nyjehnn obeyed. Dalt adjusted the overhead lamp and examined the cut on his lower lip. He glanced at his eyes.

"You're not Shaull, and certainly not O'Nel."

"No." Nyjehnn could tell him nothing more.

Dalt nodded. "Well, it's not deep. You're lucky. I heard one time she lost her temper and the guy lost his front teeth." He stretched and turned to arrange his tray. "That collar's in my way. Take off your shirt and do something with that hair, and I'll get started."

Nyjehnn sat up and pulled off his shirt. He gathered his hair over his right shoulder and braided it, securing it again with the thong from his sleeve pocket.

"How did you get these?"

Nyjehnn flinched as Dalt traced one of the scars on his back. "It doesn't concern you." He lay down again.

Dalt took the shirt from his hands. "Oh, I think it does. It will upset Mazzad, and when she gets upset . . ." He changed the subject. "She was counting on a big seller's fee for you. Now?" He shrugged and strapped Nyjehnn's wrists into the table cuffs.

Nyjehnn looked away. "I will not be sold."

Seyone had been listening at the door, and now she rushed in and faced Dalt. "You mustn't allow it. Please, remove his finder and set him free. He doesn't belong here. Please!"

Dalt was puzzled. "Seyone, calm down. What is this?"

"Don't you see? He's not like us. Don't you know what kind of life you would condemn him to?" She was on the verge of tears.

"Seyone, do you know this boy?"

Nyjehnn said, "We met a long time ago. Seyone, it can't be undone this way. Don't worry."

She stared a silent plea at Dalt.

He answered in a serious tone. "The truth is, we're all Hendar property, aren't we? Leave me to my work, all right?"

Seyone took Nyjehnn's hand in hers. "May I stay? I'll be quiet, I promise."

Dalt nodded once and turned to his tray. He considered and rejected the usual anesthetic. He had no idea how it might affect the patient. He picked up the neural control pen.

"Don't hurt him," begged Seyone.

"It can't be helped, but it's quick." He set the pen and pressed it. Nyjehnn stiffened and went unconscious. Dalt unwrapped a delicate band of gold, tapped a code on the inset bars, and slipped it around Nyjehnn's neck.

"Why," asked Seyone.

"Mazzad's orders. You promised to be silent." He locked it. "That part about being sold? I wouldn't worry. There's something odd in the way Mazzad looks at him."

He studied his patient's quiet face, the pewter lashes and hair like frayed ivory satin. Even in this induced calm there was an elusive power in him, something to which Dalt couldn't put a name. Yet it was a power to which they'd all fallen victim. There was no denying that. He shrugged and pulled the microsurgery unit down from the gleaming octopus that hung above the table and began his work.

PETAL THE TWENTY-FOURTH

It was dark outside, finally, and the snow had stopped. Brace was stiff from the cold and the waiting. The kith had saved him from freezing, and the boots were insulated and waterproof. Cintha sat huddled beside him in the dry crevice.

"Brace, what do you plan to do?"

"Create a diversion and get into the second ship."

"And then?"

"Demand Mazzad to release Nyjehnn."

"No one will be harmed?"

He looked into her innocent eyes. "I can't promise that." He stood and led her down to the plain just outside the perimeter of the ships. From behind a low hill, he surveyed the area in the light of the ship's belly ports.

"Good. No guards, no sentry beams. Come on." He led her under the nearest Sprint. The ground was concave and charred. "This way," he whispered. They crouched low and ran to the small tarp mound. Brace lifted the material. "I need more light."

Cintha cupped her hands and concentrated. Brace watched, fascinated, as between her fingers pinpoint embers sparked and glowed to flame. Spinning and brightening, they became a miniature ball of soft sunlight.

"That's the best I can do," she whispered.

"That's great." He turned and peered under the tarp. "Ah, bless their paranoid hearts, the sentry system. Looks like they were going to set it up, then changed their minds, or probably put it off." He picked up one of the clips and pushed the release. A grooved cylinder popped out. He emptied half a dozen more and pushed them into a pile under the main projector. He held up the first one.

"If we can start an overload reaction in one, it will spread to the others, blowing up the whole works, and giving us the diversion we need. Do I put it in the light?"

"No. I put the light inside the object. You can't hold it. It will burn your fingers."

Brace searched the ground and retrieved a piece of branch. He broke it in half and used the pieces like chopsticks.

"Hold it between my hands," directed Cintha.

Brace did so, and in a few moments the light shrank, withdrawing into the power charge. Within seconds the warning whine sounded and the charge glowed dull red.

"Done." He shoved it under the center of the pile

and lowered the tarp. They dashed for cover. Brace swung behind a landing strut and pulled her down beside him.

"Any second now," he warned. "Cover your ears."

The blast strobe-lit the camp in blue lightning. This close, covering their ears did little good. It was seconds before they realized the ringing was the alarms from inside the ship above them. Tatters of tarp fluttered down as three Shaull emerged from the ship with fire equipment.

As they surrounded the blaze, Brace and Cintha dashed up the ramp and into the ship. Brace sabotaged the hatch lock and raided the arms rack in one swift motion.

"Wait here while I search the ship."

"No, I'll stay with you."

Together they prowled the length of the Sprint. Brace kept the weapon ready, dodging past hatchways and entering cabins in a crouch, pointing the laser at nothing. Finally, he was satisfied.

"Sweet luck." He breathed easier. "We seem to have the place to ourselves." They returned to the bridge.

There was a staccato of explosions outside the hatch and Cintha startled.

"It's all right. They can't get in." He put his good arm around her, and led her to the navigator's pit. "Sit here. The surprise is gone. I have to act now and fast."

He whirled and jumped into the pilot's pit. He put the weapon between his legs and studied the console a moment. This was a newer model. He identified the proper controls and screens and began flipping toggles and pressing lighted keys. His attention focused on the bright screens, he never noticed as Cintha stood, listened to someone who wasn't there, and disappeared.

PETAL THE TWENTY-FIFTH

The intercom was an annoying insect in Mazzad's restless dream, a blood wasp; she had always been terrified of them. It screamed past her left ear and out of sight behind her. She tried to turn, to run, but she couldn't move. She began to shake, the terror rising, waiting for it to strike. Now she saw it again, swinging around, diving toward her in its mad, flitting pattern.

Suddenly a hand came out of nowhere and snatched the wasp from the air. The machinelike drone was muffled as it burrowed into the nacre flesh of the closed fist. Bright blood welled between the slim fingers and dripped, but still the fist did not open to release the death.

Mazzad recognized the hand and the steady voice above it.

"This will not harm you."

She woke, bad-tempered and cursing, her finger on the button, "What is it?"

"Dalt. I've finished with the prisoner."

"Why bother me? Return him to the cell."

"I think there's something you should see, first. May I bring him to your cabin?"

The dream had left her confused. She thought for a moment. "No. Not here. I'll come there."

She buckled the belt of her uniform as she strode down the passageway and entered the medbay. Dalt's quick gesture invited her behind the table. He had sent Seyone away.

"Sit up," ordered Dalt.

Nyjehnn didn't respond. He seemed hypnotized by the light of the overhead lamp.

Dalt prodded him. "I'm done. Sit up and show her."

Nyjehnn's eyes flicked to Mazzad as he moved to obey. But she caught the look. It was definite dismay. He sat up, his back to them. Dalt pointed out the scars and she understood.

"Flawed." She snorted. "Worthless. I couldn't get a half-keta piece for him anywhere." She hipped her hands and came around the table searching for other blemishes. She saw a plum bruise over his ribs, then the thin red line on his mouth, all that remained of her outburst.

"A neat job, Dalt," she complimented.

"There won't be a scar."

"Good, good. Well—" She changed her mind. "Not that it matters much now." She paced in front of Nyjehnn, thinking. "Still, you may be of some use. I might keep you myself. Such an unusual slave would make quite a stir at court. Or maybe I'll kill you in the cage, after all. What do you think?" She remembered he couldn't speak. "Ah yes, the collar. How's it fit?"

"He knows," said Dalt. "He tried to thank me." He handed Nyjehnn his shirt.

He ignored it, looking preoccupied for a moment. Then he smiled as if he'd come to an obvious decision and made a motion asking to speak.

"You've changed your mind?" asked Mazzad.

Nyjehnn nodded.

The Pack Reeve fingered the penlike control and smiled to herself. At least she had the pleasure of this power over him. She pressed the button.

The sudden release of the collar's effect made Nyjehnn cough. He massaged his throat and spoke in a husk-dry voice.

"If you . . ." He cleared his throat and tried again. "If you promise to come alone, I'll take you to the O'Nel."

Mazzad's eyebrows shot upward, then crinkled in suspicion. Why alone, she thought, and where. It must be near, he had no ship. "And if I make no promise?"

Speaking was easier. "If not, the power to release my life is not a thing casually done, but it is easy."

Mazzad smirked at him. "That's a stupid admission to make to an enemy."

"Perhaps." He added quietly. "To an enemy."

She rubbed the bridge of her nose, wondering. "What's to keep me from forcing you into it just to watch the spectacle?"

With a tilt of his head, he said simply, "You care."

Her mouth dropped open, moved, but no words issued. Her face reddened. Finally, she blurted, "Never!" She raised her hand and almost struck him again. "You . . ." She broke off, sensing that he had deliberately provoked her and she had responded. No one used her. She raised the pen in his face and pressed it.

His hand came up and guarded his neck uselessly.

"I'll see you pay for that," she hissed.

A muffled explosion shuddered the deck beneath them. Mazzad started, surprised, then touched the remote intercom on her belt.

"Bridge. Report."

The pilot replied. "The sentry projector exploded, Pack Reeve. I've sent Ship Two personnel out to investigate."

Mazzad headed out. She turned and pointed at Nyjehnn, claiming his attention. "Later." She looked at Dalt. "Put him back in the cell." She left.

Nyjehnn slid off the table and stood. Dalt came beside him and held out his shirt again.

He said. "I don't understand who you are, but don't hand your life over to her. She enjoys destruction, of any kind."

Nyjehnn took his shirt and looked into Dalt's eyes. ("Choose life, Jessan, at any price?")

Dalt stepped back, startled and confused. The prisoner hadn't spoken, but the words echoed in the memory of his hearing. He felt paralyzed by the question; it was his own philosophy.

"Yes," he managed, despite his awe. "How did you know my first name?"

Nyjehnn donned his shirt and leaned against the table. His thought was sad. ("You've touched me. I know more about you—and Mazzad—than I want to know.")

There was a disturbance, then, in the light of the room, and a tall, platinum-haired girl stood before them. She took no notice of Dalt but ran to Nyjehnn and they embraced.

At that moment, an explosion rocked the ship, throwing Dalt to the deck. Nyjehnn and Cintha held the table. Dalt scrambled to his feet as the ship's alert began wailing.

"I have to lock you both in the cell."

Nyjehnn looked at him. ("We'll be leaving.")

Dalt hesitated. "Are you taking Seyone with you?"

("Yes.")

"Go, then." He left for the bridge on the run.

Cintha touched the band around Nyjehnn's neck inquiringly.

"Marce and Willa are coming. Are you . . . ? Seyone?"

("I'm all right. Yes, Seyone's here.")

Surprise and wonder banished the tense lines in her face. He took her hand, opening her sight, and led her from the medbay.

Seyone was running toward them. She wrapped her arms around Cintha, crying. "It's not a dream. You're really here."

Nyjehnn embraced them both. He spoke in Cintha's mind.

("I want you to stay with her.") He turned toward the bridge.

PETAL THE TWENTY-SIXTH

Acrid smoke, warning lights, and jarring alarms; the bridge was filled with confusion. Mazzad was leaning over the weapons pit, checking damaged systems and shutting down the alarms. Dalt was examining the pilot, who lay slumped over the smoking navigation console. He was dead. Nyjehnn came and helped Dalt move him to the deck. Mazzad straightened and turned as the number two overhead hummed and blinked to life.

SCREEN TWO, SHIP TWO, read the Oncom digital display.

Brace's grim blue-and-white features filled the screen.

"... hear me? Can you hear me, Pack Reeve?"

"You! You treacherous slug." She brought her fist down on the console. "What do you think you're doing?"

"What I have to do. Your ship won't make orbit, now. I've taken care of weapons and long-range communications. Surrender Nyjehnn or I'll make this ship just as useless."

"Surrender who?"

"Your prisoner."

She looked at Nyjehnn, who stood calmly watching the screen. She turned to Brace again.

"You're an idiot. Destroy both ships and you strand us on this dirt ball. All of us," she emphasized. "I don't really think you'll risk that. You're bluffing."

Brace leaned into the screen. "I'll admit, I thought about leaving you here, but..." He stopped, realizing it was too late, he'd revealed too much.

Mazzad was fast. She drew her shoulder weapon and lunged for Nyjehnn. She pulled him to the screen, the gun at his temple.

"YOU surrender or I'll kill your friend." She sneered the last word. "Don't move," she instructed Nyjehnn. "No, don't look at me." She pressed the gun into his flesh. "I swear it, O'Nel. I'll kill him."

I'll kill him, ill killhim, illkillhim; her words echoed in a sudden acoustical change in the air on the bridge. A deep vibration shook the atmosphere, tingling the hairs on their skin, rising to the lower threshold of hearing, an almost sound, yet remaining mostly subtonal, a pressure resonating in the psyche.

The Nordawv, Marce, stepped into the cabin, his four arms uplifted, his mouth open. The carefully pitched sound came from his throat, a projection matched to the tonic ratio of the planet, mesmerizing music in major thirds. It amplified and the biological rhythms of the Shaull slowed in conformity to their well-remembered genesis. In the depths of their planet's voice, no thought of movement existed; Mazzad and Dalt and the lanceman stood like trees.

On the screen above Mazzad's head, a slim hand reached from behind Brace and cut the audio circuit.

In Ship Two, Brace swung around to see Cintha and a shorter dark-haired girl, who was holding her hand.

"What's going on?" he asked.

"Watch," said Cintha. "Marce knew this moment would come to Nyjehnn. He's doing what he can to protect him."

He turned back to the screen and saw that the end of Mazzad's gun was beginning to quiver. He remembered the feel of Nyjehnn's power. Part of him trusted that power, part of him wanted to surrender in case it didn't work. He felt helpless, yet there was nothing to do but wait.

Beside Mazzad, Nyjehnn closed his eyes and wrapped himself in quiet force. This was his one chance, and to succeed he must turn her against herself. He wrapped his hand over hers on the gun, sank slowly to his knees and looked up into her eyes.

She flinched as if cut by the black ice of them. Pulled within, she found herself on the violent road of her past beside a hauntingly beautiful being, as bright and terrible as a mythic messenger. It was her prisoner. He brought her to the first crosscurrent of her life and said, "Look."

It was the day her family had abandoned her.

She was walking fast behind her uniformed parents, pulled along by the mute slave who held her hand. They boarded the Tube that would take them halfway around the Ring to the military training complex. When they were settled, her father had turned in his seat and hissed, "Stop crying. You're embarrassing us. I swear, if you disgrace the family name, we'll disown you. We'll see you sent down."

She cringed; "sent down" meant the surface, meant horrible death. All the monstrous deformities and beasts stalked there. Her childish mind believed it and she fled in terror, staring out the window, blinking rapidly to stop the tears as the Tube sped callously forward.

They left her at the terminal. After four years of childhood, living on the edges of their indifference and the cruelty of their slaves, being acknowledged only at court to reap the King's approval, they had turned her over to the military without a backward glance and the person she thought of as Mazzie Hendar went away, too.

Now she was back, and there was war between the two selves. The battle raged and she was on both sides, but she couldn't be. She must choose. The old choices were back, rising unleashed from hungry adolescence. Which Mazzad would she be? She could feel her young, innocent self reaching again for love, for a chance to live. No, never, she cried. No one loved that you.

But Nyjehnn had found her, and made her relive that denial, how she had turned her back on her very core, how she had accepted, finally, the lie that in order to survive military life one must become an enemy to her soul.

He showed how her determination came from vengeance. She had excelled at hubris and strategies. With each step of rank she sensed that younger self sadly locking the doors of possibility against any return. She ran past them and knew fear, a fear that the choices she had made destroyed the real Mazzad. What she had built in her place was as much a creature of civilized savagery as every other Hendar.

She had set out to deny her parents, to rise

beyond their power. Instead, she had become a mirror. Whatever I did, it was necessary; she had told herself that often. But it was easier to pretend not to see, and so, not to question.

Nyjehnn forced her to look. And seeing, finally, all the lies between inner and outer, it filled her with revulsion and anger and a helpless pain. There was no longer a question to kill the man before her or not. She couldn't do it. He wasn't the one who deserved death.

He turned to her then and said. "It's not too late, Mazzie. Unchoose. Open the door. Release the innocent."

"I'm not Mazzie anymore."

"She's still there, waiting. All you have to do is choose. Be your true self."

"I can't!"

He regarded her, sadly. "That, too, is a choice."

She denied the hope he offered. She was too tightly bound with the double chain of fear and desire. Fear that the price would be too high. Wouldn't she lose everything she'd fought so hard to obtain: status, power, wealth? Yes. And her desire for these things was too great. Lost inside, she searched for a way to survive her own hatred. There was only one way. She twisted the gun out of Nyjehnn's grasp and raised it to her own head.

"No!" Nyjehnn grabbed her hands and pulled. The charge went off, striking the Oncom screen. They were showered with sparks and shattered glass. The coagulating vibration ceased, and Marce was between them suddenly, wrenching the gun away. He stepped back and lowered it warningly at Dalt. With his two right hands, he separated Nyjehnn and Mazzad.

Freed from her, Nyjehnn slumped to his knees. His cheek bled a single trickle of dark blood. Willa came to tend him.

Mazzad gestured at Dalt and the lanceman. "Shoot them!"

Dalt shook himself and measured the armed Nordawv. "No."

The lanceman held his arms away from his body.

Silently, she veered around Marce and headed for the hatch.

Dalt blocked her way. "No. I know what you're thinking."

"Yes. Eki-ji. We cannot give the enemy our knowledge, nor our ships. It's our final duty." She backed up.

"No self-destruct. I choose to live."

Mazzad pulled her boot knife and lunged at him. "Traitor!"

Dalt sidestepped and grabbed her knife hand. He twisted and pushed her against the inner bulkhead. She brought her knee up fast, but he threw his weight back and pulled her off balance. They both hit the deck. Dalt lost his grip, and Mazzad scrambled to her feet. She was a step away from the lanceman. She took that step, plunged her knife upward into his solar plexus and out again, turning back to Dalt before the body hit the deck.

Dalt gained his feet, still unarmed. She struck at him and he jumped back. She forced him back again, but he danced toward the open hatchway, out of her reach.

"Surrender," he panted. "It's useless, even if you win."

"Shut up, coward!" She lunged again. He knocked her knife arm aside and grabbed her wrist, applying pressure, trying to keep her knife from descending into his chest.

Brace appeared in the hatchway. He hit Mazzad on the side of her head with the butt of his laser. She fell to the deck and lay still. Dalt leaned against the bulkhead to catch his breath.

"Thanks," he said to Brace.

Brace leveled his weapon at him.

Cintha entered behind them. "No, Brace, he's a healer."

Dalt nodded toward the lanceman. "He needs attention."

"All right."

Dalt knew at a glance the man was dead. He knelt and took Mazzad's vitals; she'd have a headache when she woke, nothing worse. He took her control pen and rank rings, then moved toward Nyjehnn. He held up his hands for Marce.

"I'm a medic."

Marce nodded, lowering the gun.

Willa had finished repairing the cut on Nyjehnn's face. Dalt used the pen to unlock the collar and removed it.

Nyjehnn raised his head and opened his eyes. "Thank you," he managed to whisper.

Dalt took another device from his belt. "I'll remove the finder, too." When he'd finished, he helped Nyjehnn to stand and asked, "What happened? Everything seemed an illusion. What was that huge consciousness?" He looked at Marce.

"Remember it," answered Nyjehnn. "It was the truth."

Dalt nodded, still confused. He slipped off his rank rings and held them out together with Mazzad's. "It's not a formal surrender unless you take these."

"I don't want them." His voice was still husk-dry.

Brace approached and dropped the Sulish. "You deserve the reward. If I hadn't seen it, I wouldn't have believed it possible, not with a Shaull."

Cintha laid a hand on Brace's arm. "Please, you don't know how much it hurt him to do that."

Nyjehnn moved toward Mazzad. "You have your

freedom, Brace, and transportation home. I have my life back. That's all the reward I want." He looked down at Mazzad's quiet features. She seemed younger. There was a hint of sultry beauty about her eyes and mouth. If her hair was longer . . . He saw another Mazzad, petite and hopeful with a young girl's visions and beliefs.

Dalt offered the rings to Brace. "Shield Officer Jessan Dalt, Jagar Fleet."

Brace saluted him formally and accepted the rank rings.

"Keftain Brace TelRden, on behalf of the O'Nel-La Republic." Hearing the name aloud brought back his homesickness and his need to return.

Just then, there was a loud metallic-sounding thunk from under the ship. The deck trembled. Dalt looked surprised.

"That sounded like the shuttle dock release."

"The crewmen from ship two," said Brace. He went to the command console and switched on the dock eye. A rumble shook the ship as he watched the small private shuttle streak away. "It's armed and we're not. Let's get to the other ship, and fast."

Two sighted Cizrenhi and five passengers. Nyjehnn hesitated. "Cintha and I can take you and Mazzad. But Willa cannot take both Dalt and Marce."

Brace said, "Let her take Marce. I'm quicker, I'll run across. Just have the hatch unlocked."

In seconds, all but one were safe aboard. Brace dove through the hatch as Nyjehnn opened it. Out of breath, he gasped. "They're not turning to engage us. They've probably already alerted the patrols."

He settled in the pilot's pit and had them airborne as Nyjehnn understood his point. Brace didn't dare return to the Keep, now. He would be giving away their location.

Brace clipped on a headset.

Nyjehnn sat in the navigator's pit and did the same, monitoring the Sulish transmission. They were spilling the whole story, but there was no answer.

Marce came and touched Nyjehnn's shoulder. "I've put the medic and the commander in the prisoner cells. Willa has taken the girls home. I think we should go also. This is Brace's world. He can take care of himself. You've done your Guardianship duty."

He pulled off the headset. "He's not out of danger yet."

"He'll never be out of danger until both sides tire of playing with this illusion. You know that."

"Yes, but it doesn't mean I stop caring. I'll stay awhile."

"Are you water in the rock?"

Nyjehnn looked up into Marce's kind eyes with a sad smile. "Mazzad was a hard rock. I cut a dangerous channel."

Marce disagreed. "That was her weakness, not yours. There's nothing more you can do."

"Still, Brace stayed for me when he had a way off-planet, even when there was nothing he could do."

Marce couldn't counter that. He settled on his haunches beside the navigation console.

A loud squeal burst from the headset in Nyjehnn's lap.

Brace yanked his set off and swore.

"What was that?" asked Nyjehnn.

"Interference—from somewhere close." He adjusted the volume. "It's jamming the shuttle's communications." He cut the bridge lights and nonessential systems. With the cabin dark, and the blizzard behind them, the night stars filled the wide transparent bow shield. The shuttle's running lights blinked red and amber ahead of them. It was a blue dot on the Oncom monitor.

Another blue dot appeared on the screen, traveling on a collision course with the shuttle. Brace checked his own scope; the sensors were clear. He looked up and saw the two dots connect in a blinding explosion.

"Hoa!" he exclaimed, and pulled the ship to a higher altitude, his eyes on the scope.

"What was that?" asked Nyjehnn.

"I wonder. Friends of yours?"

"Refugees?"

"It's very probable," said Marce.

Brace banked the Sprint in a wide one-eighty. A larger dot appeared on the monitor. It looked to be completing a sweep and heading at slow, back along the course Brace and the shuttle had traveled. Brace matched their speed. The automatic recognition display read, WING-CLASS SPRINT, MODIFIED.

"Refugees," confirmed Brace. "Bet my inheritance on it."

Nyjehnn looked from the screen to the ship hanging in the night sky below them. "Wouldn't they know we're here?"

Marce leaned forward. "Why don't you see if there's an open mind on board?" He nodded toward the ship.

The Cizrenhi looked at the Nordawv, then smiled slowly. "For the sake of the O'Nel?"

"And for your own good."

Nyjehnn accepted that with a nod and turned to the Sprint. He stretched out his left hand, almost touching the inner surface of the shield, and closed his eyes. His hair fulled as he concentrated. A few moments passed, then, "Yes . . . Refugees . . . not the same group." His voice ranged higher, echoing the mind he was touching. "It has to be there. Where there's a shuttle, there's a Sprint."

Nyjehnn withdrew his hand. He smoothed his hair and opened his eyes. "They're after salvage." There was a note of awe in his voice. "Not all their equipment functions. They tracked the shuttle by its transmitter. They're brave yet reckless; the way of people who have a mission in life. I wish them luck." He looked at Brace. "They're not aware of us."

Brace was impressed. "I wish I could do that."

"You wouldn't if you knew the price."

"What price?"

Marce replied. "The illusion of your freedom to perform actions autonomously."

"What does that mean?"

Nyjehnn gestured past the shield. "When you know her as a person with the same conscious thoughts as yourself, with two young sons, whom she loves dearly, with laughter and tears and hopes and dreams, how can you kill her? She has become a part of your Self and if you managed to end her life, you would experience her death. How long do you think you could go on killing yourself and live?"

"If it was in self-defense . . ." argued Brace.

"Who is defending against whom?" Nyjehnn shook his head. "You would feel the fear she has for her sons, her fierce desire to live, a desire as strong as your own. What a lie it would be, saying your life is more important than hers."

Brace stared out the shield, thinking.

"No," said Nyjehnn. "You would not want my 'talent.' "

"Oh, oh." Brace pointed. "They're swinging around. I think they've discovered us."

He reached to switch the weapons to pilot control.

Nyjehnn's hand was there first. "No. I forbid it."

PETAL THE TWENTY-SEVENTH

Brace confronted Nyjehnn over the weapons pit.

"They'll blow us out of the sky, just like that shuttle."

"No. They need this ship."

"I need this ship."

"Then run for it. But you'd be risking five lives."

Brace stood his ground a few seconds more, then conceded. "You and your choices."

The ship-to-ship released a burst of static, then a female voice called, "Attention, unidentified Wing." The Refugee Sprint had made an inside loop and was now above them. "Attention, we have you on our weapons screen. Identify."

Nyjehnn gestured to the headset. "Tell them who you are."

Brace shrugged. "I doubt they'll believe me." But he opened the channel and said, "Don't fire. This is Keftain Brace TelRden of the O'Nel-La Republic."

The static was gone. "An O'Nel?" Off-mike she said, "Those City bugs were telling the truth, maybe." She returned, louder. "Keftain? This is Kiter Office Pont. We'll need confirmation on that."

"What kind of confirmation?"

"I'll have to insist that you put down at your previous coordinates. I warn you, any attempt to run will initiate an automatic attack sequence."

"Understood."

They were nearly on top of the old landing site. Brace turned on the running and landing lights. He brought the ship down in a wide smooth spiral and landed beside Mazzad's sabotaged Wing. The Refugee Sprint landed also. Pont came on the ship-to-ship again.

"Please leave the landing lights on. Leave all weapons on board and disembark."

Brace stood and looked at the Nordawv. "What will they think? Nyjehnn, maybe you and Marce should go. I'll be all right, now. If they're against the Ringcity, like you said, they'll see I get back, won't they?"

"We can hope they'll be cooperative," said Marce.

Nyjehnn handed Brace his kith and put on his own. "My responsibility for you doesn't end until you're off-planet and safely on your way home." He studied on the control console. "Which is the outer hatch release?"

"I don't want you to be responsible for me. I can take care of myself." He pressed a green-lit key. "It's this one." Down the passageway, the outer hatch hissed open.

"Just tell them we're friends," said Marce. He turned to go.

"Better let me lead. We don't want to scare them." Brace donned his kith. "Put your hands in the air like this as you walk down the ramp."

"Why?" asked Nyjehnn.

"So they can see that you're unarmed. And don't make any sudden moves. If you get an itch, don't scratch."

The three disembarked from the Sprint onto the brightly lit stubble of frozen ground between the three ships. Two Refugees stood waiting, bulky amp rifles slung from their shoulders, dark silhouettes in the frost and fog of the ship lights. Their breath steamed the cold air.

The shorter one approached. She wore rumpled fatigues, two sizes too big, with the sleeves rolled up, and round, wire-rim glasses. She had a cap of tight red curls and freckles across her nose. She looked harmless, but her rifle contradicted the illusion. Oblivious of the cold, she searched Brace and Nyjehnn, opening their kiths with the barrel of her rifle and shining her handlight in their faces. She came to the four-armed Marce.

"What's this—a pet?"

"Yes," blurted Nyjehnn, taking Marce's hand. "He's mine."

"Who are you?"

Brace recognized her voice. "He's a friend, Kiter. I've been stranded here and he's been helping me. Couldn't we talk inside? It's freezing out here." He lowered his arms.

She stepped back. "Yeah, all right." She called behind her. "Jaffie, check out the Wing." The other woman moved to obey. She eyed Nyjehnn suspiciously as she jogged past him. She was pale, with feathery blond hair, cut short. She was dressed like Pont.

Brace said. "There're two prisoners on board. They're mine. They surrendered formally to the Republic."

"That don't mean jerk down here." She motioned them toward her Wing with the rifle. "Inside." They preceded her into the Refugee Sprint.

It was outdated, second-hand, and rigged with modifications of older equipment. Brace marveled that it flew as well as it did. He understood why Nyjehnn said he admired their courage. They needed nerve to fly junk like this.

"On your right," directed Pont.

They entered the mess lounge. There was a fold-down table and benches. The overhead had been stripped off, revealing ducts, cables, and bare lights. There were flight maps on the bulkheads overlaid with yellowing acetate, and an Oncom screen showing the landing site outside.

"Make yourselves comfortable." Pont unslung her rifle.

Jaffie's excited voice shrieked over the intercom. "Pont, you won't believe it! We got ourselves a Hendar! That Pack Reeve on Griffin's list, Mazzad Hendar."

Pont looked at Brace with a new respect. "How'd you catch such a big fish?"

"Well, she caught me first. . . . It's a long story."

"Should I bring them over?" Jaffie asked.

"They're not going anywhere. Who else we got?"

"A medical shield officer."

"Check out the other Wing." She brought her attention back to her guests. "Sit down. So you turned the tables on her?"

Brace and Nyjehnn sat at the table. Marce began snooping through Nyjehnn's pockets, playing his role of ignored pet.

Brace answered Pont. "I had help," he looked at Nyjehnn, "but it was something like that. Look, I've got to get back to my base in the Storme Tides. I'm overdue and my information and my prisoners are vital to the war."

"I can't decide on that. You'll have to talk to Griffin. He's the senior officer. Right now, I need proof that you're O'Nel and not a trick."

"Ask me anything."

"Hold out your hands, palms up." She produced a hand scanner from a thigh pocket and ran it over his palms. The circuitry embedded there glowed blue beneath his skin, then faded. Pont relaxed a little. "Okay, you check out. But who's your friend?" She indicated Nyjehnn. "He doesn't look O'Nel or Shaull. And isn't that . . . thing kind of big for a pet?"

Nyjehnn smiled and said. "He's harmless. So am I." He held out his hand to her. "My name's Nyjehnn Kathen Dh'exai."

Pont shook his hand. She relaxed completely and smiled. "I'm Deon Pont, kiter rank, World Refugee Corps."

Marce held out his upper hand, in a shy imitation.

Pont smiled and shook it briefly. "I guess it's all right to take you back to base." She spoke to Brace. "You'll have to do your negotiating with Commander Griffin. I'm just a mechanic."

Jaffie walked in, out of breath. "Someone sabotaged weapons, communications, and the orbit boosters on the downed Wing."

"I take it that was you," Pont said to Brace.

"I needed to impress them." He shrugged. "It'll still fly."

"There're two dead bodies on the bridge," added Jaffie.

"I'm sorry about that," said Brace.

Pont gave him a puzzled frown. "So what? They were the enemy, weren't they?" She ordered Jaffie,

"Dump them overboard and pilot the Keftain's Wing."

Jaffie left and Pont turned back to Brace. "You can fly the damaged one. We can keep in touch with a remote. I'll escort your friend." Her glasses rested on Nyjehnn a second. "So don't try cutting out, Keftain, or I'll push him out the hatch, along with his—"

"Nordawv," supplied Nyjehnn, helpfully.

"Whatever." She gave Brace a two-way remote. "The sooner we get out of here, the sooner you can see Griffin. Just follow my dust." She pointed at Nyjehnn. "You stay put."

Brace stood and waved a salute at Nyjehnn. "I absolve you of any responsibility," he said seriously. He wanted to say more, but didn't have the privacy to speak openly.

In answer, Nyjehnn shook his head.

Why must he be so stubborn? Brace scuffed his boot as he walked down the ramp and toward the Wing. Well, if things went by the book with this Griffin, maybe he could requisition a ship, and Nyjehnn would have a free conscience. And then he could have a free conscience, Brace thought.

He entered Mazzad's Wing, uncomfortably aware that his circumstances were dangerous for Nyjehnn and Marce. He traveled a hazardous skyway, and had done so all his life. But up until now, it had been only his life on line, and he hadn't minded the risks, most of the time. Now, he wasn't alone. There were others, and he worried about them. What worried him most was the feeling that Nyjehnn had no concept of the peril. He acted as if this were a game. Didn't he know it could be fatally dangerous to underestimate the savagery of an enemy?

Maybe Nyjehnn knew something that he didn't. What had happened between him and Mazzad? From outside it looked like a contest of wills, and Mazzad had lost, and attempted to take the coward's penalty. It had surprised him that she had tried to kill herself. Then, he realized he knew absolutely nothing about the Pack Reeve. She was simply an enemy, an opposite, a caricature of authority, a nonperson.

That first night, in Nyjehnn's Keep, he had accused his rescuer of not knowing the reality of war. Now, for the first time he questioned his own reality. Who were these facades that he had created for his foes? Was it really a lie, an excuse to kill? Was Nyjehnn right—there's no such person as enemy?

He sat in the pilot's pit, the throb of the engines under him, and watched Pont take off, then Jaffie. He opened the throttles and followed them into the sky.

He couldn't settle his mind on an answer, not yet. He still had too many questions. If they weren't enemy, who were they? They killed his loved ones, destroyed his peaceful life, held hostage his future, tried to enslave his body and mind, and did enslave others. That was the truth. By what right did they do these things? Autonomy, that was Marce's word; the performance of independent acts for the sole benefit of the self. According to Nyjehnn, it was a psychic blindfold that allowed violence. But it not only did not benefit the self, it led, ultimately, to one's own self-destruction. Was removing the blindfold really as easy as making a choice to see?

He sat up straighter; they were approaching a volcanic mountain range. Rivers of orange lava flowed down the black flanks. The remote on the console beside him chirped. Pont's voice sounded brighter.

"Stay close. We're going to do a little canyon carving. How good are you?" she dared.

"Don't worry. I'll keep up." He thought about challenging her to a test of skill but thought better of it. He didn't have that much experience in these things. The responses were slow. In a Starfish there was no sense of flying a machine; you were the flight. The wings were your wings, and power was a thought away.

They threaded a climbing gorge, flying by lava light. Up and over the top, they banked south and dove into another channel of molten rock. The turbulence hit them like a shock wave. Brace fought to keep the nose down as they skimmed the glowing river, following its blind snake-twists between tall canyon walls, leaving it as it dropped into a smoking fault. They pulled up in a loop and rolled over, still heading south.

Pont came on the mike again. "What a ride! Still with us, I see. Well, the tour's over. We'll be landing underwater, so you'll have to convert . . . Oh, jerk it! You fixed the main boosters, didn't you? Well, use the shuttle's mains. It'll be slow, but we'll compensate. Got that?"

"Underwater?"

"Look down and to your left." He did. This far south, sunlight reflecting from the Ringcity in the southern night sky was far brighter than any moon. Below him, nested in a mountain peak was a large, crater-shaped lake spangled with silver light.

"Sanctuary Lake, we call it. Local lore says it doesn't have a bottom. Not true, of course. We live on the bottom."

They'd been slowing during Pont's speech. They passed the lake with its steep mountainsides, and banked east.

"Normally we maintain channel silence this close to base, but a short range remote is pretty safe. Watch your airspeed on the way down. You should be at near hover mode just as you hit the water, then convert. Our underwater chutes are just like space chutes, so that shouldn't be a problem. Any questions?"

He couldn't think of anything. "No. Ah, how's Nyjehnn?" He wondered what a Cizrenhi thought of this method of travel.

"Hey, you'd think this kid never flew in a Wing before tonight. He's up front with me. Here, say something."

She must've handed the remote to Nyjehnn; his voice came on channel, sounding reassuring and casual.

"Brace, you do this all the time?"

Where'd he hear that line before? Then he remembered his shocked reaction to Cintha disappearing from the library that first night. He came back, "No. If it bothers you . . . ?"

Nyjehnn laughed. "See you later."

Brace grinned and shook his head. Then it dawned on him that this was the first time he'd heard Nyjehnn laugh. It made him feel better, for some reason, gave him more hope that everything would work out for the best.

"Final approach," warned Pont.

They came in from the east, the mountains rising sharply. They flew through a pass and skimmed the surface of the lake. Brace slowed his speed, and one at a time, the three ships disappeared beneath the water.

PETAL THE TWENTY-EIGHTH

The approach lights surrounding the landing chutes came on in the last minutes, three rings of incandescent blue in the watery darkness. They entered the tubes and the hatches were secured. The water was pumped out and the inner hatches opened.

Brace disembarked into a huge hangar cave. It seemed bright after the Sprint's bridge. He looked up and saw only every third light in the geodesic ceiling was lit. He wondered if they were conserving power. Despite the illumination, the place hummed with energetic motion. Remote containers swung overhead and two-man deck rovers crisscrossed between the ship's bays. He walked down the ramp. Pont stood waiting with Nyjehnn, Marce, and a lean, sandy-haired man in white coveralls. He held a clipboard stuffed with papers. His stance favored a lame left leg.

Brace halted, uncertain. "Are you . . . ?"

He extended his right hand. "Keftain TelRden? Welcome to the World Refugee Corps, Sanctuary Base. I'm Commander Griffin, senior officer and chief tactical advisor. As I was telling your friend," he indicated Nyjehnn, "I'm an O'Nel, too, on loan from Orbitbase One. Nice to meet you."

Brace shook his hand, at a loss for a moment. He hadn't known there were any O'Nel on Julle besides himself.

"Where're you from, originally?" asked the Commander.

"Toshin Cay, sir," answered Brace, "I was born in Yyerlos."

"A southwesterner. What're you doing out here?"

"Trying to get home, sir."

He waved his clipboard. "You can drop the sir. We work pretty closely down here, and rank doesn't help all that much."

Pont glanced behind her at an advancing group and tapped the Commander on the shoulder. "The prisoners, Griffin."

Jaffie and two guards presented the Shaull officers at gunpoint. Mazzad was steady and smoldering. Dalt stood behind her, looking around the hangar. They were both in wristcuffs.

Pont said, "The Keftain claims they belong to the Republic. I told him he'd have to take that up with you."

Mazzad tested her bonds. "I am the Grandarch Mazzad Hendar. I surrendered to no one. I belong to no one. This traitor," she jerked a thumb over her shoulder, "is guilty of mutiny, theft of a superior officer's rank rings, and conspiring with the enemy for the overthrow of the Dynastic State."

Griffin reappraised Dalt. "Is this true?"

"Yes," admitted the medic. He sounded tired.

Griffin smiled and gestured at the guards behind Dalt. They nodded, unlocked his wristcuffs, and closed ranks behind Mazzad.

Mazzad fumed. "I demand he be executed by the laws of the Eki-ji code."

Griffin ignored her outburst. "Take the Grandarch to the brig." Jaffie and the guards led her away.

Griffin shook Dalt's hand. "What's your name?

"Shield Officer Jessan Dalt, medical class."

"Good, we're badly in need of doctors, if you'd consider joining us. We're all mutineers, conspirators, and enemies of the State, and we have our own code."

"I hadn't planned on what happened. I don't know how things turned out the way they did."

Brace stepped closer. "When I came in, he was unarmed and fighting her for his life."

Griffin checked the time on his clipboard. "Let's hear the whole story over breakfast. It's about that time." He glanced out over the busy hangar, noting the place of each man and machine, a habit, but performed in an un-self-conscious way that told much about his careful leadership. He signed the top paper on his board and gave it to Pont. "Take these to the hangar chief and join us down-level." She saluted and left. Griffin led the newcomers to the elevator, its doors emblazoned with a sun symbol.

Nyjehnn entered beside Brace and got his attention with a touch. He inspoke. ("It's almost dawn. I've got to get away for a few minutes without being missed.")

Brace stared at him, wide-eyed for a moment, then nodded.

The doors opened again and Griffin led the

way—his limp was slight—down a darkened corridor. There was a green stenciled design lining one wall, a lone tree repeated endlessly.

"Pardon me Commander," asked Nyjehnn, "why is it so dark?"

Griffin answered without looking back. "We use a day/night cycle down here, as much for economy as for our sanity. We've even found it healthful to institute weather in some parts of the complex. Like the artwork?" He gestured at the stencils. "It was the children's idea. Now they can recognize each level easily, especially the little ones who can't yet read."

Brace was walking beside the Commander. "You have children down here?"

"They're safer here than on the surface." He sounded grim. "We don't have to worry about losing them to the slavers. Despite the so-called treaty, the Shaull still raid the surface colonies." He halted at a wide doorway on their right. Inside was a gymnasium-size cafeteria, filled with regiments of tables and benches. In the back was a kitchen, all gleam and steam and busy with cooks. Griffin pointed to his left. "There's the men's lav, if you need to wash up. I'll see to the food."

Nyjehnn and Brace went into the lav, leaving Marce to watch the door. Nyjehnn removed his kith and unbraided his hair.

"I'll be right back." He disappeared. Brace took off his heavy kith, too, and hung them both on the wall rack. He used the facilities and washed up, including his hair. He saw they had a shavex and started to vacuum up his growing stubble.

Nyjehnn came back, looking younger and fiercely bright, his ivory hair full. He stood with his eyes closed for a moment, breathing deeply and stretching. He ran his fingers through his hair, quieting it, and opened his eyes.

"It's fantastic up there this morning. How can these people choose to live underground like this, away from the sun?"

Brace dried his face with a soft paper towel. "You heard Griffin—they must hide to be safe."

Nyjehnn rolled up his sleeves and washed his hands and face. "There's a better choice for them, if they could dare it."

"What?"

"Train the children and let them be taken." He dried and started to braid his hair again.

"That sounds so cruel, especially coming from you."

"It would be a sacrifice, yes, and you wouldn't see results for maybe ten, fifteen years, but that kind of infiltration has the best chance for success and the least probability for war."

"You sound like Marce."

"He was my teacher."

The door slammed open, startling them. Griffin stood with a guard behind him. His hospitable manner was gone. "You." He pointed at Nyjehnn. "You'rc under arrest. Out." He stepped back for the Cizrenhi to exit.

Brace followed. "Wait a minute. He's a friend of mine."

Griffin eyed him. "Are you a telepath, too?"

Jaffie stood behind the guard. "No. It was the thin one. He was in my mind when we were sent out to intercept the Wings."

"What've I done wrong?" asked Nyjehnn.

Griffin motioned the guard to handcuff him. "You're a threat to our security. I'm sorry, but you must be confined. If you attempt to escape, you'll be killed."

Brace stepped between Nyjehnn and the guard. "I can't allow this. He's on our side. He saved my life twice. If it wasn't for him, I'd be a Shaull prisoner right now, and you wouldn't have two new Wings for your fleet, or your Hendar hostage."

"I've only your word on that. I'm not saying I don't believe you, only that it doesn't matter. If he can gain any fact he wants simply by reading a mind, he's dangerous. The Shaull don't suspect us, and I have to keep it that way."

"He's not a spy!"

"How do you know that? How long have you known him? Where's he from? Who is he? He's not one of us." He said to the guard. "Take him to the brig. His . . . companion, too." He nodded to the Nordawv, who was still huddled by the door. "Stand aside, Brace."

Nyjehnn glanced back with a warning. ("It's not important. Concentrate on getting your passage home. I'll be fine.")

Brace had already seen the futility of trying to convince them. He didn't have Nyjehnn's talent. They would believe what they chose to believe until they chose to believe differently.

Griffin put a hand on his shoulder. "I hope this isn't going set us against each other. You're military; certainly you can see I'm doing what I feel is right for the Corps. I still want to hear your story. You could tell me about him."

Brace straightened. "He told me once, he can't read a mind that shuts him out. But that's not important now. It's more important that I get back to my base in the Storme Tides. In fact, I think the outcome of the war may depend on it, if it isn't already too late."

They sat down to breakfast together—Griffin, Pont, Jaffie, and Dalt—and Brace told them about his mission to gather intelligence about the report of a new Shaull base in the Tides, which if true would be a direct violation of the truce. He found the base on a remote asteroid, melted into the carbon and ice.

They were building giant dual-flow boosters, larger than the star sevens on their Vedettes, but for what? He was captured before he could find out.

Brace went on to tell about the crash on Julle and his rescue by Nyjehnn. No he didn't know where he was taken, which was partly true, he couldn't remember, somewhere in the northern mountains. He told the entire story, right up to their meeting with Pont and Jaffie, which according to Jaffie, was Nyjehnn's fault, unless he didn't know he would give away their presence. Pont added that telepath or not, he seemed a very sincere boy.

"Yes," added Dalt, "I doubt he's a spy. At first I thought he was a plant, but now I have the feeling he deliberately diverted Mazzad to himself."

Brace nodded. "I tried to talk him out of it. He said he was tired of running, whatever that meant."

For some reason that reminded Dalt of the cadet/assassin. "I have something here from one of your people, I think." He patted various pockets. "Here it is." He displayed the rank ring Seyone had given him. "He was a keftain. He madc an attempt on Mazzad's life. He's dead. I'm sorry."

Griffin took the ring reverently and handed it to Pont. She stared at it with a dry-eyed, hopeless sorrow.

"He was her brother," explained Griffin. "He volunteered for a strike mission. The choice of target was up to him."

"He died quickly," said Dalt, "by his own hand—Eki-ji."

"Thank you," whispered Pont. She got up woodenly and left. Jaffie went after her. Dalt stood, thinking he might help.

"That was kind of you," said Griffin.

"It was the truth. He cut his throat in the cage." He left.

The Commander paled and stared at nothing for a moment.

"We'll hold a ceremony for him tonight. I don't mind admitting, sometimes I get damn sick of this hiding, living like bats, flying strike-and-snatch raids. This is a heroic group of people. I've no complaints. They're amazing. I wish I could do more for them. But I also wish I could get back to the Tides." He turned to Brace. "How long've you been out of intertie?"

The question caught him by surprise. It was a matter between keftains. Then he remembered Griffin was from Orbitbase One.

"Not long, about four days, I think." Thinking about it brought back the vision of scintillate wings skimming the stars. It made him ache suddenly for the sleek power and freedom of flight. He stretched his fingers.

"Sorry," said Griffin, looking away.

What had he seen in Brace's eyes? Everything, to someone who knew the experience—another linked O'Nel, a keftain.

"How?" asked Brace. He meant, Griffin was a base commander, how did he survive the loss of his ship? How did he continue to survive without that tie? It was like losing a part of yourself.

A shiver lifted Griffin's shoulders. He looked down at the table with a sensitive frown. "It was an accident . . . running the Twists . . . a long time ago." The Twists, that brutal cacaphony of gravitational forces that had spun out braided rings in multilayers of the Storme Tides. They were treacherous to fly and forbidden by official orders. But, unofficially, they were the elite's rite of passage, a keftain tradition. Brace had taken the risk, and had come through. Griffin had not.

"I'm sorry, Griffin."

"So am I." He shrugged, distractedly, and sighed. "I know someone who can tell us all about what's going on in the Tides. We'll ask the Pack Reeve a few questions." He stood and stepped away from the table, picking up his tray.

"Questions that she won't answer," added Brace, as he stood.

"We'll see."

PETAL THE TWENTY-NINTH

The lake bed was called Fish Level, and contained acres of gardens and aquaculture ponds, divided by a flume array of hydroturbine power plants. The next floor up was Hand Level, holding manufacturing and processing, supportive services, and social correction. Then came Tree Level, which was residential, education, and medical care. Ram Level was military training. Hawk Level was judicial, administrative, and intelligence. And Sun, the top level, was the flight deck. The detention cells were on Hand Level.

Nyjehnn and Marce were taken to the cell next to Mazzad and locked in. Nyjehnn's wristcuffs were not removed. He knew the guards were afraid to touch him. His cubicle was a four-meter-square mirror image of Mazzad's: a bunk, a latrine, a bolted pedestal table in the corner, a ewer of water and a cup, and a chair.

Mazzad was lounging on her bunk, her uniform jacket open. The white shirt underneath warmed her light-olive features. She smirked at Nyjehnn. "Well, isn't this cozy?"

"In a way. I did want to talk to you."

"You've done enough 'talking.' Just leave me alone." She avoided looking at him, speaking to the air in front of her.

He leaned against her bars, testing their reality. "Do you know what they plan for you?"

"Oh yes, but it'll be a waste of their time."

"What?"

"A negotiation. But we don't trade; besides, the family'll be overjoyed to be rid of me; all the more for them. When these grubs find they can't use me, they'll execute me."

"Why?" Nyjehnn couldn't follow her reasoning.

She laughed harshly. "Why? Because that's what we do to enemies. That's the way we keep score. Those who live, win; those who die . . ." She rubbed the bridge of her nose.

"You don't want to die, Mazzie." Despite her desperate attempt, he knew the truth. She had only wanted an end to the part of her that was conflict.

"Don't call me that." But she didn't sound angry; she sounded resigned.

"I can save you. Would you like to go home?"

She gave him a sour look. "That's not funny." She made a flick of her wrist to indicate her cell. "In case you hadn't noticed, we're in prison. By the way, why're you here?"

"They're afraid of me."

She nodded. "They should be, you're a dangerous weapon."

He was silenced by her analogy. It was an odd viewpoint, to think of himself as a weapon. And if he was, by whom was he being used? For what purpose was the weapon called Nyjehnn being wielded? He spoke to Marce without turning.

"Is this true, Marce?"

"No. It's only to those who need secrets that truth is a danger. Remember her place." His voice was deeper and rumbly among all the metal walls, like wind in a chambered shell.

Her place, not physically, but emotionally, psychologically, her entire personhood up to this moment. He knew her almost as well as she knew herself, better in some ways; he wasn't caught in her self-deceptions. And for that, she considered him a weapon. In her eyes, she was right.

There was the clang of bolts being throw open and footsteps in the corridor. Griffin and Brace and a guard stopped outside the cells. Brace came to Nyjehnn's side.

"I'm sorry about this. I tried to talk to him, but . . ."

Nyjehnn smiled. "Don't worry."

Griffin opened Mazzad's cell. The guard went in first. The O'Nel commander came in, holding a videocam. He trained it on Mazzad a few moments. "For the folks back home," he said.

Mazzad hadn't moved from her bunk. She glanced an "I told you so" look at Nyjehnn. Griffin put his camera on the table, brought the chair over, and sat facing her. The guard kept his weapon ready. Griffin called Brace in. The keftain came and stood inside the door; cells made him nervous.

"We'll relay that little piece of transmission along with a request for the return of certain children taken from a mining colony recently. Your family can see that you're alive and well. If they value your continued longevity, they'll cooperate. If not . . . the next transmission will be of your execution."

"Then kill me now, and save yourself the time and trouble. A Shaull in enemy hands is given the rites. We do not bargain."

"I'm sorry for you."

Mazzad sneered at him and looked away. Nyjehnn was in that direction. Every time she looked up, his dark, penetrating eyes were piercing her. It was as if he were her lover, waiting for her on a street corner while she gave directions to a passerby. Then they would continue their stroll. She almost smiled at such an inappropriate fantasy.

Griffin watched her carefully. "Next item of business is the construction project in the Storme Tides."

She eyed Brace a second, but said nothing. She felt strangely detached.

"Yes, your ex-prisoner. We'd both like to know what such large engines are meant to power."

Now, she did smile, a small secret smile, and said nothing. She looked toward Nyjehnn. But the fantasy was gone. He stood with his face hidden in his hands. She heard him gasp.

Brace came to him. "What's wrong?"

Nyjehnn ignored his question. He raised his head and stared in horror at Mazzad. "No. . . . How could you even think of doing it? It's insane. . . . So many innocent people!"

Brace reached through the bars and put his hand on Nyjehnn's shoulder. "What is it?"

"The engines . . . they will—"

"Shut up, you freak!" Mazzad was on her feet.

Griffin held her back. "They will what?" He demanded.

"They will send . . . asteroids to O'Nel-La to destroy—"

"Oh my God," whispered Brace.

"When?" asked Griffin.

Nyjehnn took a deep breath to regain his composure. "Soon. I don't know." He concentrated. "They're waiting for something."

"A launch window," guessed Brace.

"Get out!" screamed Mazzad. She twisted in Griffin's arms. "This was set up, wasn't it? You knew I wouldn't talk, so you put him in the next cell."

Griffin threw her on the bunk, motioned Brace and the guard out. He hung the videocam on his belt loop, and locked her cell.

Mazzad jumped up. "It's too late, you know. There's nothing you can do to stop it now. The system's ours!"

Griffin unlocked Nyjehnn's cell, and personally removed his cuffs. "I'm sorry I put you through this. I had no idea it would be . . . Are you all right?"

Nyjehnn nodded hesitantly. "Water?"

Marce was already bringing a filled cup from the table. Nyjehnn reached for it, but his hand shook. Brace steadied it while he drank.

They helped him out of the cell. Marce followed quietly.

Griffin said, "We'll find someplace quiet where you can lie down a bit and rest."

Mazzad taunted them. "Yeah, better take good care of your little mental pickpocket. Bastards!" She yelled after them.

Nyjehnn seemed dazed. They took him to a darkened room in the intelligence section of Hawk Level, and laid him on a couch. Marce settled on the floor beside his head and held his hand.

Griffin closed the door quietly and said to Brace.

"You have your ship, and anything else you need." They strode toward the central operations room. The corridors were bright with the day cycle and, busy with efficient personnel in pressed fatigues.

Brace tried to sound calm. "She's probably bluffing about it being too late, don't you think?"

"Let's hope so. I'll notify the other bases immediately, but it'll take time to get through to O'Nel-La. The Shaull keep the space channels pretty well shut tight."

They entered the modest communications center. It was small by Brace's standards, and there wasn't a light optics wall map, but the fact that they managed to keep lines of communications open under the noses of Ringcity's Cencom was a major triumph.

"If Reed were still alive, it'd be easy. He could always slip a packet out for me under their own grams."

"Reed? Oh, Pont's keftain?"

"Yes." Griffin leaned over the girl at the first station. "Find Dvorik. Tell him to meet me in my office, immediately. And get the hangar chief. I want a Wing readied."

He looked at Brace silently for a moment. The young man was waiting, nervously, roaming the room with his eyes. He tried to think of a few words to offer, but realized there was nothing adequate to be said. He could easily imagine the worldwide devastation that would result from a hail of precisely aimed giant meteors, and knew that Brace saw it, too. Their eyes met, and Griffin smiled bravely and patted him on the back. They left together for the commander's office.

In the small, quiet room, Nyjehnn stared at the ceiling.

"Marce?"

"Yes, Kathen."

"It's too dark to think about."

"Yes."

He sat up slowly, folding his legs under him, lotus fashion.

"I must warn Aunt Morthena. I . . . I don't have a sunball."

Marce reached in a lower pocket and brought out a small one. He placed it in Nyjehnn's palm like an offering, and began to hum very low. Nyjehnn gazed into the sunball. The dark crystal globe flickered with pinprick sparks that gradually brightened and spun to a golden radiance. Nyjehnn and Marce were illumined in their close orbit of this mystic sun; their shadows loomed like dark, silent guardians on the walls surrounding this private universe. The base and its peoples and its desperate needs were Outside.

Nyjehnn took deep breaths and let the last one drift away without him. Marce began the pretrance intonations.

"Relax. . . .

"Release. . . .

"Reclaim. . . .

"Remember. . . .

PETAL THE THIRTIETH

Griffin's office was frequently used for staff briefings, base meetings, and morale ceremonies. It was large and there were chairs around the outer wall, a desk, and a player for video tapes. The back wall was covered with a large map of the Rethyann Solar System. Lights around the room were indirect to put the more formal gatherings at ease.

Griffin fiddled with his videocam while he waited for Dvorik. He'd come to know the younger second-in-command during his twelve years as advisor, but he couldn't say he knew him well. Dvorik kept much of his personal life and his past private. Yet Griffin knew enough to predict how he would react to his news: disbelief. He inspected the lens of his camera.

Brace sat beside Griffin, elbows on thighs, watching people pass by in the corridor. One thought kept looping through his head: these are Shaull. He knew it wasn't rational, they weren't Those Shaull, but he still felt uneasy among them. It was probably just nerves; he felt a real pressure, almost a panic, to get home. Time was too swift sometimes.

A tall, rugged man with skin the color of light bronze entered the room. His hair was brown, which gave him a strange monochrome presence, except for the brilliant teeth in his smile.

Griffin stood up. "Dvorik." They shook hands.

"What's the problem, Griffin?"

"This is Keftain Brace TelRden. He's just out from the Storme Tides. I'm afraid we've some very grave news."

"Keftain." Dvorik shook Brace's hand with a frank look of serious calculation. Brace knew this was a man who never made snap judgments, a man of quick intelligence. He had the confident, clean charisma of a natural leader.

Griffin pulled over a chair. "Sit down, Dvorik. I've some tape I want you to see." He put the videocam into the playback unit under the wall screen and dimmed the lighting. He started the tape. Mazzad filled the screen, reclining arrogantly against the wall of her cell.

"What?" Dvorik glanced at Griffin.

The commander paused the film. "Yes, Pack Reeve Mazzad Hendar, Grandarch and now, with the recent assassination of Dern Hendar, second in line to the Dynastic Throne. We have her in custody."

"Since when?"

"This morning." He started the film again. The scene moved back, and the angle became wider. Griffin entered the camera field, taking a chair and sitting in front of Mazzad. Everyone in both cells could be seen, except Brace, who, at the door, must've been out of range. Griffin turned up the sound and said, "I want you to pay particular attention to the platinum-haired young man on the far right of the screen. He's a telepath."

They sat in absolute silence as the replay aired. It made Brace edgy to watch it again. As the film came to Nyjehnn's revelation about the true objectives of the Shaull's presence in the Tides, Griffin stopped the tape. The last words were Brace's, "Oh my God." It hung in the room, the echo of everyone's mind.

Griffin brought Dvorik up to date. "What you've just witnessed occurred in the brig on Hand Level not thirty minutes ago. Briefly: this morning, before you came on duty, we acquired two Shaull Wings. One was piloted by a recently escaped POW, the keftain here. The telepath had helped him escape. The Hendar was in their custody. Of course, in the interest of security, I've detained them all."

Brace became wary. Griffin had promised him a ship and the freedom to leave. Was he going back on his word?

"Let's see the rest," said Dvorik. When it'd played out, he nodded. "So now we know the truth about the big push. At least it's not directed at us, as we'd feared. What do you have in mind, Griffin?" He propped his right ankle atop his left knee.

"We don't know their timetable, but the Shaull are planning to launch inhumane weapons against the O'Nel. It could destroy the entire population. We should mobilize immediately and send a warning, if it's not too late." He glanced at Brace. "We should make a formal declaration of war against the Shaull, and our first act should be a public trial and execution of the criminal responsible for the attack: Mazzad Hendar."

Dvorik lifted a hand in objection. "Now wait a

minute. I realize your sympathies are heavily involved, but I've got to think of the Corps. We're not prepared for all-out war, not now."

"We don't have the option of a long, secret siege anymore."

"I disagree. It's taken years to build our Underground. I'm not going to see it destroyed for partisan revenge."

Griffin was insulted. "The Pact you signed with the O'Nel-La Republic specifically states that you will send reasonable aid in exchange for technology and advisors."

"Fine. I'll send as many ships as I can spare to the Tides, but I'm not going to launch an offensive against Ringcity. It would be suicide." He added, "And you know it."

Griffin sat back. "All right. It might be too dangerous at this time, agreed. But at least strike back. Use the Hendar. She's valuable. Get as much for her as you can, if you can. If not . . . show them you're serious."

"We don't even dare do that. We don't need them on the alert. We can't survive another full-scale Refugee hunt."

"So what are you saying? The lives of millions of O'Nel on the brink of extinction, and you're going to do nothing?"

"Griffin, we're grateful to the Republic for their support. We'll do all we can, all that's possible. But we won't be annihilated for you. I can't believe you'd want that."

Griffin stood up and turned off the player. "No, of course not." He rubbed his forehead.

"There's a lot we can do. We'll try to discover the launch date. If they've been launched, we'll find some way to stop them, or divert them. I'll send ships and crew to help you fight. We can even start an evacuation . . . just in case."

Griffin was sober. "Evacuate to where?"

"Here," said Dvorik. "Julle. There's certainly room enough."

"I want prevention, not evacuation." He sat on the edge of his desk. "What about the Hendar?"

"She was on our list, anyway. She'll be killed where they can find her—with the usual misleading clues."

Brace spoke up. "Officially, she's my prisoner. I have the rank rings to prove it."

Dvorik studied him silently, with a sidelong look.

Griffin said, "As senior officer, you should've surrendered them to me when I took custody. What with the confusion, this morning, it's understandable. Do you have them on you?"

"They were in my parka. I left it down-level."

"I'll have it sent up. They're important to us. There're places you can't gain access to on Ringcity unless you have a rank ring of some sort."

Dvorik stood. "They took yours when you were captured?"

Brace looked at his bare hands. "Yes."

The second-in-command looked anxious to get back to duty. "Well, Griffin, I'll inventory the fleet and see what we can send. You'll want to get a message out. Who do you want to assign to the Hendar, or do you want the job yourself?"

Griffin was staring at the solar system map. "I'll leave that to you. I'm thinking it'll be just as fast to go into the Tides as send a warning. I've already got a Wing on standby. I'll go back with the Keftain here."

"Without official orders?"

He looked at Dvorik. "Under the circumstances, yes. I feel confident about leaving you in command. You're a fine officer." He held out his hand, and Dvorik shook it.

"Thank you. Good luck then." He turned to Brace, who stood with them, and shook his hand. "You're the first real keftain I've met, other than Griffin. It was an honor. Safe flight to you both." He saluted and left the room abruptly.

"Like I said, a good officer—not an easy man, but a top-grade officer." He took the videocam out of the player, and removed the tape. "We'll take this with us. I've some things to clear up. I'll meet you on Sun Level in say . . . an hour. Bring your friend, too." Griffin left the office.

Another hour, thought Brace. He should check on Nyjehnn. He walked closer to the solar system map. It was computer-generated, accurate in its scaled detail. O'Nel-La was a lovely turquoise and white opal with a silver-pearl moon. It was unthinkable that anyone would have so much hate as to deliberately want to destroy such fertile beauty.

"Yes." Nyjehnn's voice was behind him, speaking Dhoran. "It's madness." Brace turned. Nyjehnn and Marce stood in the center of Griffin's office. They both looked insubstantial amid the soft lighting. Nyjehnn came to the wall map. His hair glowed under the brighter light of the ceiling spots.

"Remember I told you I had a link on O'Nel-La?"

"Yes."

"I've spoken with her." He looked at the map, and lifted his delicate hand to trace the wide orbit of the Storme Tides.

Brace felt a flutter of hope. "You've warned them?"

"I warned her. She's searching for a mind that holds the knowledge of destruction—the time and the path." His hand dropped to squeeze Brace's shoulder briefly. "We'll help you. This must not happen."

"You're coming back with me?"

"That isn't necessary. We have our own ways."

Brace nodded. "Thanks, Nyjehnn, for everything." There was silence between them for a moment. It occurred to Brace that he might not see Nyjehnn or Cintha ever again. "Are you leaving?"

"Soon. I've one more responsibility."

"What's that?"

"Mazzad. They plan to kill her. I can't allow that."

"How will you . . . ? Oh." He remembered that Nyjehnn wasn't dependent on any of their primitive methods of transportation. He could easily free her. "Be careful, Nyjehnn."

"I will. You too."

"Say good-bye to Cintha for me."

"No."

"What?" Brace was puzzled by his refusal.

Nyjehnn smiled. "We never say good-bye; we can't. You'll never be separated from us, never be lost again. You're Inside, now, no matter where you go."

"Inside . . . ?

Nyjehnn pointed to his heart. "Inside. You are known, and cannot be unknown." He held out his hand, and they shook on it. "Lady's Grace. That means: 'Peace, until we speak again.' "

"Lady's Grace then, Nyjehnn."

The Cizrenhi walked back to the Nordawv, who lifted his left hands in farewell. Nyjehnn took his upper right, and they disappeared suddenly. It was as if Brace had blinked, but he hadn't. Nyjehnn's handshake left a warm feeling in him, like the deep surety of intimate friendship, a companioning that didn't seem to be fading. Everything around him looked familiar and nonthreatening. It was the same room, but he saw it differently, and he wondered at that for a long time.

PETAL THE THIRTY-FIRST

Nyjehnn stepped from an adjacent dark hallway and stood contemplating Mazzad. She lay on her bunk, one booted foot on the floor, tapping arhythmically, and one arm over her eyes to keep out the harsh light. The tapping paused and she sat bolt upright, staring at Nyjehnn ouside her cell.

"What'n the hell are you doing here?"

"I came to help you."

She sprang up and strode to the bars. "I don't need your kind of help, and I don't want anything from you. Go away."

"They're coming to kill you in a few minutes."

She straightened her uniform. "An officer is always prepared to give her life. It's the Eki-ji way."

Nyjehnn shook his head admonishingly. "You can't lie to me, Mazzie. I know you. You're not ready to face a death like this."

"What is it with you? You save lives for a living or something?"

"As a matter of fact—"

"So . . ." She kicked the cell door. "You've got the key?"

He looked down at the lock. "No. I don't need one."

"You pick locks as well as minds."

Nyjehnn smiled. "No." He concentrated on the area behind her. Then, he was behind her, standing inside the cell.

Mazzad whirled around and stared at him in utter disbelief. She looked outside the bars again, then back at him. "This is some kind of trick," she stated. "You're not there. It's a projection." She reached and pushed against his chest, testing his solidity, then backed away, perplexed.

"You chased me halfway across the continent, yet I had no ship. How did you think I traveled?"

"I dismissed it. I had more important things on my mind."

"Do you want to go home?" he asked again, reaching for her hand. "I can free you."

She swallowed, remembering the intimacy of his touch, and backed along the bars. "Don't touch me." She came to the table, groped and hefted the heavy metal ewer, never taking her eyes off him. She held it like a club, standing now, with her back to the wall. "I can't trust you."

"It's not me you don't trust."

"You see? That's why you're so dangerous. You use a person like they were a sword pointed against themselves. It's wrong."

"Why?" He took a step closer.

"Because . . . I don't know. It's just wrong!"

"Why is it wrong?" he insisted, and took another step.

"Because, if I'm fighting myself, I can't fight you!"

Nyjehnn stepped in quickly and pinched her wrist. The ewer dropped with a clang. He held her hand.

She struggled to control her breathing. "Let go of me."

"No. Why must you fight me?"

His question echoed in her until, finally, it found the answer. "I'm afraid of you."

"Yes. Because you don't know me. But that's changing now, isn't it? You know now that I care about your life. I've only goodwill toward you. We have much in common."

She did feel different. He was changing her, somehow. Telling her things without words, using snatches of special memories, recalling people in her past that had truly cared about her: an old slave woman, a young lover who'd been killed in the early years of the war. He used wisps of tender emotions. But whose? "Is this what I feel, or what you want me to feel?"

"Trust yourself, Mazzie. It's the truth. You want to live unharmed by me, and I want to live unharmed by you. We are not enemies—we want the same things."

She understood what he was saying. It sounded so simple, yet so profound. And it was truth. His dark eyes were close and soft as midnight velvet. She was pulled in and they stood again on the road, but it was leading in the opposite direction. It no longer led to her mutilated childhood, but to her future. She saw herself standing in her apartment. It was a starlit city night, one of the few real nights of the year on Ringcity, and she had friends over for a party. (She did not have friends.) There were couples dancing on the transparent floor of her living room, dancing on the racing clouds, and friends laughing and toasting her. But she did not have friends.

"Is this a dream, or real?"

"It's a possibility. It's your choice."

The party, and laughter, and clink of glass faded, and they stood together in the Refugee cell once again. Nyjehnn caught a faint, distant sound. He stepped back and let go of her hand. He began the transference, concentrating with a part of his mind on the sunrise point he'd used earlier. Marce was waiting there.

"They're coming." His voice was hushed, but urgent. "Do you want to go? Answer me."

Mazzad went pale at the sound of the outer bolts being thrown back. The Eki-ji code monotoned its strict duty through her head. "I can't! It's cowardice."

Nyjehnn became exasperated. "It's survival!"

Two guards came into view. They saw him and gave a shout. They raised their weapons toward him.

Mazzad grabbed Nyjehnn's outstretched hand. "Yes!"

They disappeared in a flicker of light.

The light became sunlight. It was noon. The high air was chill and the blue-green, mountainous carpet flowed down from under their feet in serried hills and darker folds. It ended, on their left, at the Altjiam Ocean, with its chalk-white beach, and stretched to their right, to blue indefinition, upon the horizon.

Marce sat nearby, perched on a flat shale rock.

"Where are we?" asked Mazzad.

Nyjehnn pointed up. All three of them looked upward to the silver-blue city hanging above the puffy clouds. It shimmered like a crystalline mirage.

Mazzad had never seen it from this viewpoint. There was an aspect of enchantment to it. Nor had she seen that the surface of Julle was so beautiful, and harmless. There were no monsters. The air was sweet, almost heady. Or was it the escape that made her feel so buoyantly free?

She clung to Nyjehnn's warm hand. Outwardly, he was her opposite in every way: a different race, an unknown history, a being with unexplainable abilities, yet, inwardly, she knew who he was. He was without deceit. He was now, as she was then—at five—an innocent child. In his touch, they had spoken heart to heart, and he had reminded her how to be that self again. It was easy. And it was hard. But it was life. And she felt more alive, at this moment, than she had in all her past twenty-five years of walking around pretending.

Nyjehnn leaned toward her. "Ready?"

The sunlight blazed. When she could see clearly, she was standing in her apartment, looking down at the white clouds below her feet. Nyjehnn had let go of her hand and was inspecting the room, noting the chrome stair railing and the soft gray carpet.

"I live here sometimes," she said.

"It's nice."

She looked around. "But . . . too serious."

"There's nothing wrong with serious. It's quiet. I should go, Mazzie. Marce's waiting."

She became more somber and nodded in agreement. She tried to think of a suitable reply but couldn't; she had no practice in small talk. Instead, she said, "Thanks."

"Try to be happy." He smiled and disappeared.

She drifted to stand where he had stood, and looked down at the distant surface of Julle. So much had been transformed in so short a time. Julle was not what she thought it was. Her prisoner was not who he was supposed to be, but someone she needed to find. And now, she was not who she had been. Pack Reeve, Grandarch Mazzad Hendar, second to the Throne; these were tendencies. They had never been deliberate actions, but reactions. They were never truly her. It was such a relief to know that, to be free of them.

Be happy, be happy; his last words sang a mantra in her mind. She looked around her empty apartment. The trick will be to stay free. The first thing I'll do, she thought, is change this to remind myself. I'll change everything. But what about her family, her duty, her plans? I'll resign. I'll start over. I'll get to know Mazzie again, and she will tell me what she wants. The new Mazzad wasn't naive; she knew it wouldn't be easy.

PETAL THE THIRTY-SECOND

Nyjehnn stepped out of the sunlight and went to Marce, his ancient Nordawv teacher and friend, who still sat patiently on the shale rock. They regarded each other for a silent moment. Then Nyjehnn laughed with relief and threw his head back with an audible sigh.

"I did it, Marce. I did it!" He laughed again and hugged the big Nordawv as best he could.

Marce put his four arms around Nyjehnn and rumbled a grateful, "Naturally."

Nyjehnn leaned back. "And I could do it again. I'm a real Guardian now, like my father and my grandfather." Marce released him and he jumped on the rock, and then to the next one in the jumble that lay there, and sat down with another laugh.

Marce chuckled deeply and rumbled on, a great purring, base staccato of perfect delight.

They sat together, watching the surface of Sanctuary Lake, and watching hawks sketch graceful circles in the wind, and waiting for the last leave-taking.

The sudden whine of a Sprint engine split the alpine air. A Wing rose from the lake, and arced south over them and dissolved into the bright sky.

Nyjehnn watched it go. "That was Brace," he said.

He had his final reward. The O'Nel was on his way home. That reminded him of the danger that awaited Brace's home world, spinning around the inner sun, unaware of the impending destruction. It was inconceivable to him that the Shaull would plan and attempt the annihilation of half their own race. Setting themselves apart from the O'Nel by using the word "Shaull" didn't change reality. They were one leaf on the tree of the Self-conscious universe. If half the leaf is struck off the remaining is forever aware of its missing part, and mourns secretly, and sickens, and eventually dies too.

But it wasn't yet a matter of destiny. Neither Morthena, himself, nor the other Guardians had been touched by any hint of wrongness in the stars of Outside. The last warning was when grandfather Thaj had learned of the Suaadian sun before it had gone red. Then, nothing needed doing; the Aixerthon had already been preparing for centuries. Marce had said it was a matter of mutual evolution—planet and people—together. It had been a destiny they had chosen to take for their own reasons.

Here, everything was still on the path of choices. And Nyjehnn felt confident they had time. It was a good feeling. How long since he'd been this sure of life? Six years since the tragic end of the first Keep, since his father's death. Among all the rest, this was what Nyjehnn had lost; not his life, but his confidence that he was worthy to live. Now that specter was gone. He felt free, cured of a long illness. He pulled in a great lungful of new mountain air, and breathed out the old.

He turned to Marce. "Let's go home."

PETAL THE
THIRTY-THIRD

Cintha and Willa, Khast and LeAnn held hands as they stood under the ruined temple eaves. Dawn had been late, having to climb above the heavy violet clouds that were crouched over the northeastern hills. The sky was magenta cream, forecasting the coming winter storm.

Cintha said the ritual words as they came out of Sunning.

"Zehl jerra Wey." She turned her back to the icy wind. They all turned away, their cloaks fluttering and snapping, then they were gone, taking the sound with them.

They materialized in their sheltered courtyard and folded back their dark hoods.

"He should've been back by now," muttered Cintha. "A few hours—Marce promised."

Willa rubbed her cold hands. "It's been only a few hours. It's a wide continent. If there was trouble, he would've sent word. Come inside. It's going to snow." She led Cintha toward the Common room. Khast and LeAnn followed. Bright sunball light welcomed them from the open doorway.

Seyone was waiting there, next to a pillar. She was dressed Cizrenhi fashion in a lavender kimono under a darker wist, tied by a red sash. She looked supremely happy. Then, her face lit even more as she pointed behind Cintha.

There was a small whirlwind of sound, and Nyjehnn and Marce were standing in the courtyard. Cintha ran to her brother and hugged him fiercely. He lifted her off her feet and squeezed her tight, then set her down.

"It's finished," he said. "Everything's . . . light."

"Did you hear that, Willa? Success!" She tugged at his arm. "Come in to breakfast and tell us all about it. What happened after we left?"

They crossed the courtyard. Nyjehnn gathered Seyone in his left arm. He smiled at her, then hugged her off her feet, too. She laughed with relief and joy, and they went inside.

LeAnn served samp and corn milk, fruit, and plenty of hot tea. There was talk and smiles between them, and everything was indeed light again.

In a pause of conversation, Willa put down her teacup. "Let's have the Dedication, today, right now."

"Yes," agreed Khast. "It's the perfect time. What do you say?" he asked Nyjehnn.

Nyjehnn measured the determination around

the table and found it absolute. "All right. It *is* after harvest."

Willa rose, businesslike. "Preparations will take only an hour." She began to clear the dishes.

LeAnn rose to help. She looked outside and exclaimed.

"It's snowing. Khast, let's go south for flowers. We can't have a festival without flowers."

Khast stood. "I know a place where they grow almost as big as zho blossoms." He and LeAnn linked hands and were gone.

Cintha took LeAnn's place in the kitchen.

Seyone moved to rise and help, but Nyjehnn put his hand over hers on the table.

"Stay with me," he said.

Seyone settled and looked down at his slim hand. "I still can't believe I'm here with you and Cintha again. It's a miracle. I never thought it would really happen."

"Can I admit I dreamed about it, too?"

Seyone smiled shyly and studied his face, relearning the gentleness of it. "It doesn't seem like six years."

"No, not now." He thought back to those quiet, empty years of slow reconciliation and how the real healing had happened overnight. It truly was a miracle. And finding Seyone—that was an unexpected gift, and those were the best kind, the ones that brought the deepest joy.

"Nyjehnn, what is this Dedication?"

"A mutual pledging ceremony. I promise to serve as a Guardian and as a First to the people who promise to assist me."

Marce added, "A very beautiful ceremony, as I remember. I especially like the chanting."

Nyjehnn was more solemn. "I don't think there will be much chanting this time." They would have to leave out that part of the ceremony; he had no recollection of his father ever making a Dedication petal for him. That was another reason he hadn't wanted to face the ceremony. He hadn't wanted to acknowledge that truth, but now maybe that emptiness was something he had to look at to be wholly free of the past. He didn't relish the idea.

Willa came with ceremonial over-robes of white watersilk that were brushed with silver batik patterns. She laid them out on the table.

Seyone caressed the fabric. "These are lovely."

Nyjehnn stood up. "I'm going to take a hot shower first. Come on, Marce. You look a little dry."

"Good idea." They left together.

By the time Nyjehnn and Marce were finished, Khast and LeAnn were back with large pink-flower leis, and the preparations were complete. Dressed in watersilk, the excited group met in the Communatory, their private chapel under the courtyard tiles, accessible only by teleport. Willa had arranged the pillows in a circle, with Nyjehnn's pillow in the center.

They took their places. Nyjehnn faced east. Khast, LeAnn, and Willa were on his left; Cintha, Seyone, and Marce were on his right. The sunballs were quiet overhead, but someone had randomly strewn the floor with giant sunballs from the greenhouse. They illuminated the marching pictorial of the Sacred Migration on the walls around them. alien constellation patterns that had been skillfully carved in Nyjehnn's refined style. The gems that represented the Guardian suns shone like pilgrim's candles on the starry galactic way.

It was time to begin. Khast stood. As the only other Cizrenhi male, he acted as Nyjehnn's attendant. He took Nyjehnn's robe, shirt, and soft boots and put them aside. Bare to the waist, his braid over his shoulder, Nyjehnn sat again, in full lotus, and Khast returned to his pillow.

Nyjehnn watched Cintha adjust her singing drum. It always filled him with pride to see her sure independence. She began the ceremony with one strike of her beribboned drumwand. The high-tuned strings above the drumhead sang.

Willa, as the eldest Cizrenhi, began the ancient chant of pledging, each line supported by the drum's hollow beat. The others blended their voices aloud on the responses. Marce's deep vibrato supported the measured chant.

T'ahn zehl jerra Wey. T'ahn jerra zehl Wey.
O'saa prahl winna-dith. Prahl saa winna-dith.
Zocen txan avil cavoni. Txan avil cavoni zocen.
Zo Jenn.*

*He-one, a truth from Light.
We pledge always our Forever Song.
We speak with our being complete. We bless.

The last word resonated with the drum strings, rising away like a soul in flight. The Cizrenhi opened their hands toward Nyjehnn, palms out. He breathed deep, accepting the small gifting of personal energy each sent: Willa's motherly caring, Khast's strong admiration, LeAnn's shy adoration, and Cintha's devoted love—all sent with the blessings of the Lady.

Cintha removed the wand ribbon from her wrist, stood, and came to her brother. She lifted the porcelain vial of fragrant Tl'anwa oil from the lacquer tray in front of him and knelt. She didn't touch his mind; a First's Dedication was a very private experience, the few in their lives they hadn't shared.

Nyjehnn smiled at her and closed his eyes. She

touched the tip of her finger to the oil and annointed his forehead and eyelids with the Lady's sacred curled sign. He stayed her hand with his own and inspoke.

("If not for these eyes, you would sit here.") He meant that she had been in training for the Guardianship before him, that a freak accident had made him First in her place.

("I have no regrets,") she answered. She rose and handed the vial to LeAnn, who annointed the smooth skin over his heart. Khast signed his shoulders and hands, and Willa sealed the upturned soles of his feet.

Cintha struck one of the minor strings. She depressed the supple drumhead underneath, and the note wailed and quivered with the attendant beat. With skilled agility, she played the simple repetitive melody, preparing their minds for the next part of the ritual.

Nyjehnn sat in the familiar darkness behind his eyes. The exquisite scent of the Tl'anwa flower reminded him of the garden pools of home. It was an old memory, a happy one, before Outside. He let it fade before his father came through the fragrant hedge; he would face that loss soon enough. His heart beat faster at the thought. He concentrated on Cintha's music and calmed. The last notes left an inner harmonic threading the edges of his awareness, companioning him. He heard the fluid rustle of watersilk and looked up. Willa stood above him, and she held a knife. It was time. Yet, why go through with this part of the rite, he wondered?

Marce lumbered forward. From his upper cuff pocket he took a small furmine envelope and withdrew its treasure, a round petal. He held it up to the light and it glowed with a cloudy pink opacity that indicated it was blossomed.

Nyjehnn shivered with awe. "I didn't know he left one. You've had it all these years?"

Marce nodded solemnly.

Nyjehnn was completely shaken. He leaned forward, face in hands to compose himself. All these years he believed there would be no message. But then he'd never asked Marce; he'd been afraid of the answer. He straightened. Willa questioned him with a look, and he nodded.

She knelt and Nyjehnn held out his right hand, palm up. She steadied it with her other hand and looked at him beseechingly; this part of the ceremony frightened her. Not that she hadn't done this rite before; she had dedicated Eathan. It was that she'd never cut Nyjehnn. In all the years of service to his body since its birth, in all the months of healing, she had never used a knife on him.

"I ask forgiveness of your flesh," she pleaded.

Nyjehnn swallowed dryly and nodded once.

Willa held her breath and nicked the center of his palm. She watched a drop of dark blood grow in his hand. Marce gave her the petal. She laid it in Nyjehnn's palm, its edge touching the crimson pebble. Red bloomed at the edge and grew until the petal was the color of his blood. If it hadn't been Nyjehnn's petal, there would've been no change. But he was its catalyst; it was made for him. The petal began to shrink, dissolving, releasing its mystery, sacrificing its substance.

When it was gone, Willa swabbed his palm clean. The cut was a thin, freshly healed line. She placed a small sunball in his hands, and both she and Marce returned to their places in the circle. With LeAnn and Cintha they began chanting the Entering Mantra. Cintha kept time with a soft drumbeat.

Nyjehnn focused the thought of energy into the sunball. It blazed between his fingers. He felt the natural pull from the vortex of this mystic universe and let himself go. The glow of a thousand newly created suns surrounded him. The chanting expanded and echoed, becoming the music of his cosmos.

He waited.

The warmth spreading within him from the petal aroused strange snatches of almost-thoughts, half-emotions, fragmented memories, all tangled together and misty, like pieces of a fading dream struggling to be real in the sudden light of morning.

They coalesced.

"Nyjehnn?" A whispered echo, familiar, but a shock. A memory never remembered. Old, yet freshly implanted in him in this time, one with his flesh now.

"Son?" A shadow eclipsed the globular stars, and soft rainbows, as in Kirlian photography, fractured the solar brightness. Father sat facing son across the chasm of time and death. His hair was darker than Nyjehnn remembered, and there was stress around his eyes. The synthetic memory-image of Eathan pursed his lips.

"This moment at last," said Eathan. He made a wavering smile. "I wanted so much to be with you on this day." After a second of inner decision, he shrugged. "Something tells me I won't see the ceremony. I'm glad you're away tonight so I can do this. Marce says not to worry about you, you'll be all right." Another pause and he looked directly into Nyjehnn, the sadness unconcealed. "Custom is to share some experience of mine that I feel will help your future work. But I've nothing to give except a secret. . . . All your life, Nyjehnn, you've been my teacher. It's true. If there was some decision I had to make, or any time I wanted to know what was best for myself or others, all I had to do was look at your life—what you were doing and why.

"There's nothing I can bequeath to you except my profound gratitude that you chose to become Jenna's son and that I had the gift of knowing you in my lifetime." He smiled sadly and his voice tightened. "Tell Jenna I miss her. Take care of Cintha. Lady's Grace to you, and my love. I dedicate myself to you."

He opened his arms, palms out. The psychic force of his gift engulfed Nyjehnn, a flood that threatened his already fragile heart. Eathan's image grew transparent, his etheral lightbody dispersing. Then he was gone, and the cosmos darkened.

Nyjehnn's brimming tears fell. He didn't stop them, didn't want to deny his grief any longer; six years was long enough.

This petal was made on the night of Eathan's death; he was certain of it. He could even smell the lingering spice of that evening's meal, pepperleaf, as it mingled with the fragrant wood-paneled library of the first Keep. It brought back vivid pictures of salt beaches, Sant'kye practice on the courtyard square, lessons with Marce and laughter with Lita. He lived those years again, and only gradually did he become aware that he was in the future and the chanting in the Communatory had ceased.

He opened his eyes and saw Seyone kneeling before him. She'd been crying, too. She smiled bravely and placed the pink lei that she held in her hands around his neck. She kissed his wet cheek.

"Is it over?" she asked quietly.

"Yes . . ." he whispered. He looked at the precious faces of his sister and his friends. "Now we can begin."

APPENDIX A

THE WORDS

CIZRENHI WORDS

Aixerthon	Extinct race of Death Mystics. Their sun entered red dwarf stage shortly after the last death rite. Studies are in progress to determine if their race committed voluntary genocide.
Blackwood	Subtropical, black-stemmed frond plant, genus bambusa, native to Julle. Used by the Cizrenhi for room screens,

	lightweight furniture, boxes, baskets, hats, trays, etc.
Cizren	Translates, "Place of Beginning"; name of Cizrenhi home planet. See *Lady.*
Cizrenhi	"People of the Beginning"; racial name.
Crossing	Term for the unique method of disincarnate star travel of the Cizrenhi. Its science is strictly protected by the Nordawv Institute of Psychic Biology.
Cumber	A round, green fruit high in ascorbic acid.
Deun Keep	A nearby, out-system Guardianship Keep. The word "Deun" means journey.
Dhoran	Universal spoken language of the Cizrenhi.
Donner	Floor-length hooded winter cape made of furmine. See *Furmine; Furwood.*
First	Hereditary temporal and spiritual leader in the Guardianship network. Succession is usually reserved for the female line, traceable to the first Mother. See *Lady.*
First Emergence	First galactic Crossing in the history of the Cizrenhi race.
Furmine	Tanned inner bark of the furwood tree. See *Furwood.*

Furwood	A species of subalpine coniferous evergreen native to Julle, the inner bark of which is harvested wet. When dried and tanned, it makes a soft and durable chamoislike material prized for its warmth, suppleness, and velvetlike texture. Used for outerwear, boots, and furniture.
Guardianship	An intragalaxy outpost and communication network established by the Nordawv-Cizrenhi Alliance.
Holy signs	A highly stylistic hand-signing developed in the early history of the Cizrenhi to add nuances and personal expression to telepathic speech. As vocal speech became more evolved from its origin as music, signs became more ritualized and hence more sacred, eventually taking the role of a spiritual language. However, it became a practice to use signs more openly Outside as an ethnic tradition.
Inside	Spatial reference to the Cizrenhi home world, being within 8,000 light-years of the galactic core and inside the dust ring that obscures the outer sprial arms of the galaxy. It is also an emotional location referring to what is known, secure, and valued.
Jerra	Translates "to emerge from."

Kathen	Translates "friend, honored one."
Kith	A parka-length furmine coat with inner pockets and a combination collar and hood; lined in watersilk. See *Watersilk.*
Lady	The Divine Mother of the Cizrenhi. The personification of the Causal Mind manifesting in Cizrenhi Archtypical form. It is recorded in the crystal petals of the people that before the beginning the Cizrenhi were the dream children of the Goddess of the Universe. In order to create more perfect love, She gave life to Her dreams. She prepared a place and at the chosen dawn, Her children flew forth from Her joyful tears. This First Dawn is the central myth of Cizrenhi Migrations, and the Rite of Sunning. See *Sacred Migration; Sunning;* and *Petals.*
Lyrent	A long-necked acoustic musical instrument having a hollow oval body with five graduated watersilk strings and two harmonics.
Mornsyth	Name of the sun around which orbits Cizren. The Dhoran word means dark star.
O'Nel-La Keep	The Rethyann inner system Guardianship Keep on O'Nel-La. Nyjehnn's aunt Morthena is its First.
O'Inin	Translates "so chosen." Second part of the ritual words used to

	bond a starlink between Firsts. See *Qi'nin; Starlink.*
Outside	A spatial reference pertaining to the outer stars and beyond. Any place beyond the inner dust ring of the Milky Way galaxy. Also refers to anything not understood, frightening, or denied.
Pepperleaf	A highly pungent deciduous spice tree native to Cizren. It bears small berries which when dried provide a popular spice. The phrase "loud as a Pepperleaf forest," comes from the harvest season when the drying leaves curl around the berries just before they drop from their stems. When any wind blows, every leaf rattles, creating a loud, hissing sound.
Petal	A thin, organic crystal disk used as a biologically coded recording device by the Cizrenhi. Grown from a plant native to Nordawv. Information is recorded by the rearrangement of the crystalline structure. The message is released by dissolving the petal in blood. They can be coded for an individual or for general information.
Planetfall	The final stage of a Cizrenhi star voyage. Upon arrival at a biosphere the entity returns to its previous incarnation. Scientific information is protected by the Nordawv Institute of Psychic Biology.

Qi'nin	Translates "seeking." First part of the ritual words used to bond a starlink between Firsts. See *O'Inin.*
Sacred Migration	A cyclic compulsion in the lives of the Cizrenhi who live Outside. It was discovered by the early Guardians that they could not stay Outside indefinitely, that there was a psychic bond between themselves and their home sun; they were pulled to return periodically by some inner instinct.
Samp	Stir-fried hominy served with honey, spices, and corn milk. A traditional breakfast food.
Sant'kye	Physical and spiritual discipline taught to every Cizrenhi. It encompasses exact knowledge and control of the physical and psychic self.
Singing drum	A wide, thin drum strung with five harmonic metal strings. The drumhead is made of furmine. It is played both with a slender drumwand or by the hand. The strings can be hammered by the wand or plucked with the fingers. The drumhead is secured in such a way that the drumbeat can resonate with the strings to produce a quivering "singing" tone.
Sior	Translates "year." Does not, however refer to a planetary orbital period, but to constellation progressions.

Starlink	A telepathic level of communication between Firsts based in the widespread Keeps of the Guardianship.
Suaad	Home planet of the Aixerthon race. See *Aixerthon*
Suaadian	Only known language of the Aixerthon race. See *Aixerthon.*
Sunball	A glass sphere blown in various sizes ranging from 14 to 49 centimeters in diameter. Used by the Cizrenhi for light, for meditative preparation before starlinking, and as temporary receptacles for psychic energy prior to Crossing. See *Crossing.*
Sunning	A daily life-sustaining activity performed by every Cizrenhi at dawn. A property of sunlight is drawn into the body through the eyes. Information on this science is under the protection of the Nordawv Institute of Psychic Biology. (Warning: Looking at the sun may cause eye damage.)
Tans	Top-stitched fitted jeans made from brushed furmine.
Tl'anwa	Flowering evergreen hedge native to Cizren. Source of oil for perfumes. Flowers become inflated as they mature in summer.
Watersilk	A delicate fiber harvested from the sap of a subalpine evergreen tree native to Julle. In early summer, the branches ooze a milky

sap which dries in long, wispy falls. The fibers are gathered and soaked in running streams and combed to expose the silklike inner threads. It needs no further method of preparation other than drying before spinning and weaving into a soft, strong cloth. Used for kimonos, shirts, wists, undergarments, drapes, and bedding. See *Wist*

Wey	Translates "light." It can refer to sunlight, but also means the immortal spiritual light.
Wist	A stiff-bodiced, sleeveless overdress, usually made from watersilk. A winter season wist is made from furmine.
Zehl	Translates "truth." Refers to absolute truth.
Zehl jerra Wey	Ritual speech pattern to withdraw from Sunning. Literal translation is, "Truth from Light." The meaning is multilevel, encompassing the ideas of the primary source of all Cizrenhi, in both spirit and flesh, and their basic creed.

SHAULL WORDS

Altjia	Largest major continent on Julle. Dominates the Northern Hemisphere and spans six time zones.
Cencom	Central command and communication complex located in both the WinterRing and SummerRing sections of Julle's orbital Ringcity.
Eki-ji	Military warrior code of conduct and discipline.
Grandarch	Military nobility title of rank equivalent to lord/lady.
Half-keta	The basic monetary unit. Contains approximately ten cents worth of silver.
Jagar	Exo-canis Julle. A small, swift, carnivore mammal that hunts in packs. Characterized by large neck ruffs and bushy tails.
Julle	The Shaull's postexodus world; planet orbiting the secondary sun, Yann, of the Rethyann System.
Mect	Unit of measurement corresponding to divisions of latitude and longitude for global navigation.
Northern Dominion	Name for the Northern United Continents, the land holdings of the Shaull on the planet O'Nel-

	La before they emigrated to Julle. These are now ecological wastelands.
Oncom	The Sprint's onboard computer system.
Orbitspy	Ring-based stationary tracking and relay systems.
Rethians	Shaull term for the O'Nel.
Ringcity	The geostationary orbital habitat surrounding Julle. Composed of linked tetrahedron constructs forming a torus around the planet. It's divided into two halves named after the major seasons: SummerRing and WinterRing.
Sauradon Project	The name for the Shaull's ultimate military assault against the O'Nel-La Republic.
Sulish	Shaull language.
Tekar	Paper scrip. One note equals twenty keta.
Tidal Wars	Intersystem conflict between the Shaull and O'Nels for control of the mineral-rich asteroid ring called the Storme Tides.
Yann	Parent sun of Julle, having a mass of approximately 27,800 earths and being the second protostar of the Rethyann binary system.

O'NEL WORDS

Cliise	A fishing port off the Eastern Skerries of Toshin Cay.
Ecology Law	O'Nel Southern Dominion council formed to protect the biosphere through regulations and judicial action.
Keftain	O'Nel term of rank indicating a ship-link status with a Starfish.
Nel'A'Sheylii	Legendary semi-angelic beings said to inhabit the ice ranges of the Southern Pole during the last Tropic Age.
O'Nel-La	Name of the home planet of both O'Nel and Shaull. Term refers to planet and moon.
Orbitbase	Military launch station on the moon of O'Nel-La. Ferry point for the Storme Tides.
Reth	Planet sun of O'Nel-La, having a mass of 1,008,000; primary star of the Rethyann binary system.
Starfish	Semisentient organiform spacecraft adapted by the O'Nels from creatures found inhabiting the Storme Tides. Second of four stages of the Spacefish life cycle, which includes: young ultra-light airoform floaters, mature Starfish, neostructural podding nurseries, and megastructural habitats.

Storme Tides	Asteroid ring orbiting the inner sun, composed of planetoids, asteroids, and debris, with a total mass of less than 0.11. Composed of both C-type and S-type bodies.
Toshin Cay	Largest of the Southern Continents belonging to the Southern Dominion on O'Nel-La.
United Continents	World Governing Body of O'Nel-La, established in the year 21,315 O.E. (Old Earth)
Yyerlos	Capital city of Toshin Cay, located on the western coast; seat of Ecology Law.

APPENDIX B

SHAULL MILITARY CRAFT

1. SCOUT-CLASS SPRINT

ORIGIN: Altjia Spacecraft Center

TYPE: Vedette-based/Ring-based, single-seat, swept-wing multimission, multisensor reconnaissance, interplanetary/suborbital short-range strike fighter.

DIMENSIONS: Full wingspan 9.6 m, swept wing 7.3 m, length 12.6 m, height 3.8 m.

WEIGHT:	Fully armed and loaded, 9.2 metric tons.
ENGINES:	Two two-phase multithrust atmospheric J-Star turboramjets /dual-flow ramjets.
ARMAMENT:	Two superlaser cannons, six inbay smart missiles.
PERFORMANCE:	Maximum speed (suborbital) mach 3.0. Attack range 6000 km. Interplanetary maximum speed 90,000 kph.

---

2. SHUTTLE-CLASS SPRINT

ORIGIN:	Altjia Spacecraft Center
TYPE:	Vedette-based/Ring-based multimission transport lifeboat, long-range craft. Crew of six.
DIMENSIONS:	Wingspan 9.9 m, length 14.2 m, height 3.9 m.
WEIGHT:	Empty, full fueled, 12.7 metric tons.
ENGINES:	Two two-phase multithrust turboramjets/dual-flow Star-IV series ramjets.
ARMAMENT:	Two superlaser cannons.
PERFORMANCE:	Maximum speed (suborbital) mach 2.6. Interplanetary maximum speed 1,600,800 kph.

3. VEDETTE-CLASS SPRINT

ORIGIN:	Altjia Spacecraft Center
TYPE:	Interplanetary Starsprint, sustained mission scout carrier. Multisensor mobile space station.
DIMENSIONS:	Breadth 228.6 m, length 296.1 m, height 84.2 m.
WEIGHT:	Battle-ready, 91,600 metric tons.
ENGINES:	Four multithrust/dual-flow Star-VII series megaramjets.
ARMAMENT:	Eight superlaser cannon turrets (upper/lower), twelve Scout-class Sprints.
PERFORMANCE:	Maximum interplanetary speed 1,100,000 kph.
SHIP'S COMPLEMENT:	Five command officers, twenty-four flight crew, ten lance-grade crewmen, and seventeen slave rank.

---

4. WING-CLASS SPRINT

ORIGIN:	Altjia Spacecraft Center
TYPE:	Ring-based, interplanetary/sub-orbital defense patrol craft, mul-

	timission, multisensor reconnaissance Sprint. Six-man crew.
DIMENSIONS:	Wingspan 12.3 m, length 22.1 m, height 5.2 m.
WEIGHT:	Shuttle docked, fully fueled, 27.5 metric tons.
ENGINES:	Two two-phase multithrust turboramjets/dual-flow Star-IV series ramjets.
ARMAMENT:	Two superlaser cannons, twelve in-bay smart missiles.
PERFORMANCE:	Maximum speed (suborbital) 2.1 mach, with shuttle booster 3.9 mach. Interplanetary maximum speed 9,400,000 kph, with booster 21,000,000 kph.

APPENDIX C

SHAULL MILITARY RANK RINGS

ENTRY RANKS: *ringless*
Cadet
Cadet first rank

COMMUNICATION RANKS: *first ring (left hand, middle finger)*
Lance cadet
Lance officer
Lance reeve: adjacent ring (two rings on same finger)

FLIGHT RANKS: *third ring (left hand, ring finger)*
Cadet kiter
Lance kiter
Kiter officer
Kiter reeve: adjacent ring

SERVICE RANKS: *fifth ring (right hand, middle finger)*
Shield cadet
Shield lance
Shield officer
Shield reeve: adjacent ring

COMMAND RANKS: *seventh ring (right hand, ring finger)*
Pack cadet
Pack lance
Pack officer
Pack reeve: adjacent ring (total of eight rings)

ADMIRALTY RANKS: *ring stars (diamonds)*
Lance admiral: one star
Shield admiral: two stars
Pack admiral: three stars
Reeve admiral: four stars